Inspectors of Irish Fisheries

Inspectors of Irish Fisheries report, 1885

Inspectors of Irish Fisheries

Inspectors of Irish Fisheries report, 1885

ISBN/EAN: 9783742812322

Manufactured in Europe, USA, Canada, Australia, Japa

Cover: Foto ©Andreas Hilbeck / pixelio.de

Manufactured and distributed by brebook publishing software
(www.brebook.com)

Inspectors of Irish Fisheries

Inspectors of Irish Fisheries report, 1885

CONTENTS.

REPORT

OF THE

INSPECTORS OF IRISH FISHERIES

ON THE

SEA AND INLAND FISHERIES OF IRELAND, FOR 1885.

TO HIS EXCELLENCY JOHN CAMPBELL GORDON, EARL OF ABERDEEN, K.P.,

&c., &c., &c.,

LORD-LIEUTENANT GENERAL AND GENERAL GOVERNOR OF IRELAND.

MAY IT PLEASE YOUR EXCELLENCY,

We have the honour, in conformity with section 113 of the 5 and 6 Vic., cap. 106, to submit our Report for the year 1885, being the seventeenth since the Sea and Inland Fisheries of Ireland have been placed under the superintendence of this Department.

THE SEA FISHERIES.

The returns obtained from the Collectors of Customs and the Coast Guard show that the number of Registered Vessels in Ireland during 1885 fishing for sale amounted to 6,687, with crews consisting of 20,721 men, and 770 boys.

Of the above, 1,4[illegible] vessels, 5,[illegible] men and 337 boys, are shown as exclusively fishing for sale; and 5,2[illegible] vessels, 15,302 men and [illegible] boys as partially so engaged.

It would appear from the above that there is a decrease of 118 vessels and 144 men and 171 boys since last year.

We have, however, to repeat the opinion expressed in former reports, that these returns cannot be considered as accurate, as we are aware that numbers of boats are engaged in fishing, particularly on the west coast, which are not registered.

THE PILCHARD FISHERIES.

During the year large quantities of pilchards were taken in the nets fishing for herrings in Ballinacourty, Dungarvan Bay, and Dunmore East, County Waterford. The fish were of fine quality, but as there was no sale for them they were thrown back into the sea.

It is a matter of regret that the curing of this fish is not regularly carried on in the south of Ireland, as it has been for many years in Cornwall, where it is one of the principal industries upon which the fishermen and their families depend.

It has been calculated that Italy—to various parts of which the fish, when cured, are despatched, will take upon an average about 30,000 hogsheads per year. For many years past, the supply has fallen much below the demand, as will be seen by the following, which gives the number of hogsheads despatched yearly for the last ten years, and the prices obtained—

			s.	d.		s.	d.	
1874,	7,343½	hogsheads, prices realised from	60	0	to	85	0	per hogshead
1875,	7,337	„ „	53	0	„	96	0	„
1876,	9,203	„ „	45	0	„	100	0	„
1877,	8,477	„ „	40	0	„	80	0	„
1878,	10,809	„ „	30	0	„	60	0	„
1879,	11,357½	„ „	41	0	„	68	0	„
1881,	13,963	„ „	45	0	„	75	0	„
1882,	7,817	„ „	41	0	„	84	0	„
1884,	14,545	„ „	45	0	„	77	6	„

A hogshead contains 2,300 fish, not count, and when it is considered that a ready sale, as stated, can be found for them, it is somewhat surprising that some enterprise has not been induced to embark in an attempt to revive an industry which formerly existed in the south of Ireland.

In several annual reports we have drawn attention to the fact that great quantities of this fish frequent the southern coasts. Until the last three or four years they were to be

A 2

found off the shores of the County of Cork, but for the last two or three they have been seen in vast shoals off the Waterford coast, from Ardmore to Dunmore East.

About fifty hogsheads were cured at Baltimore in 1880, which were readily sold, they were fine and realised a satisfactory price.

The remains of pilchard curing places are still to be seen in the County of Cork, at Baltimore, and at Glengariff, and it is believed they existed in many other places along the southern coast.

THE MACKEREL FISHERY.

The capture of mackerel during the season 1885 was less than in the previous year, 1884; but, on the whole, it must be regarded as a fair season.

The total number of boxes, containing 120 mackerel in each box, sent to the different markets was 165,860, realising to the fishermen £164,684—averaging 18s. 3d. per box.

The quantity of fish landed at the different stations was as follows:—

	Boxes	£		Boxes	£
Kinsale,	67,143	65,759	Dingle,	3,608	1,957
Baltimore,	40,410	34,585	Kilcredane,	1,115	529
Ballydavid,	14,507	18,484	Ballydonegan,	6,067	3,036
Union Hall,	2,523	1,719			
Castletownsend,	1,569	3,890		165,860	154,638
Ventry,	1,716	673			

The average prices obtained at the four stations where the great bulk of the fish was landed, were as follows:—

	£	s.	d.			£	s.	d.	
Kinsale,	0	18	0	per box.	Ballydavid,	1	0	2	per box.
Baltimore,	0	17	0	"	Castletownsend,	0	14	1	"

The nationalities of the fishing vessels engaged in the fishery in 1885 were as follows:—

Irish,	270	Scotch,	41
English and Manx,	302	French,	58

The number of English and Manx boats attending the mackerel fishery has considerably decreased since 1881—whilst the Irish boats have increased in number. In 1880 there were 407 English and Scotch boats to 210 Irish. The English and Manx have fallen to 302, while the Irish have increased from 210 in that year to 270 in 1885. The Irish boats have considerably improved in the last few years. New and improved boats having in many cases been substituted for the old ones, and the value of the equipment increased considerably. It may be taken as a fair estimate that the value of a vessel with a train of mackerel nets is worth £400; taking this as the value, it would show that a sum of at least £108,000 is invested in Ireland in this industry.

The fishing commenced at Kinsale on 13th February, and ended 20th June; at Baltimore, 20th March, and ended 11th July.

There were 392 men employed in the hulks used by the buyers—at the rate of £1 5s. per man per week, this would amount to £8,330 for seventeen weeks, besides a large expenditure upon packers, carters, &c.

At Kinsale there were 12 steamers employed conveying the fish to England, at an estimated cost of £400 per month, and seven hulks for storing ice, at a cost of £45 each per month.

Six vessels arrived with ice, 3,948 tons of which were imported.

The following rates were charged for carrying the fish. To Liverpool and Manchester, 5s. per box; to London, 10s. 6d. per box of 120 fish; the average weight of a box was 1 cwt.

At Baltimore 10 steamers were employed in carrying the fish to England, the cost per month per steamer being about [illegible].

At Baltimore 154 men were employed in the hulks used by the buyers, at a cost of £1 5s. per week each; this for 10 weeks would amount to a sum of [illegible], besides a large expenditure upon packers, &c.

Three vessels arrived with ice, of which 2,400 tons were imported, and 5 hulks were used for storing it—two at a cost of £20 per month, the others were owned by a company of fish buyers, and the cost has not been stated.

The mackerel fishing has proved of great benefit in giving employment, not only to the fishing population, but to a great number of persons residing in the vicinity of the places where the fish are landed. Some years back none of the vessels engaged fished from Kinsale, but this year during the season fished from various ports between Kinsale and the mouth of the River Shannon.

There were only 53 French luggers fishing off our coasts during the late season, being a decrease of 14 as compared with the year 1884.

Piers and Harbours.

The Act 46 & 47 Vic., c. 26, granted a sum of £250,000 out of the Irish Church Fund for the purpose of carrying out these Works, and the following is a summary of the allocation of that sum for Works recommended, viz. :—

	£	s.	d.
In County Antrim, . .	1,000	0	0
" County Clare, . .	24,150	0	0
" County Cork, . .	30,800	0	0
" County Donegal, . .	26,705	0	0
" County Down, . .	17,300	0	0
" County Dublin, . .	1,879	10	0
" County Galway, . .	26,230	0	0
" County Kerry, . .	6,100	0	0
" County Limerick, . .	19	0	0
" County Londonderry, . .	4,000	0	0
" County Louth, . .	21,783	0	0
" County Mayo, . .	17,080	0	0
In County Sligo, . .	16,080	0	0
" County Waterford, . .	13,088	10	0
" County Wexford, . .	6,500	0	0
" County Wicklow, . .	9,500	0	0
	230,000	0	0
To which is to be added the sum reserved by Board of Works by direction of the Treasury to cover expenses, viz., . .	20,000	0	0
Total, . .	£250,000	0	0

The following is a list of the Applications received for grants for constructing or improving Piers, Boat Slips, and Harbours. The works are given in the order of counties, and not of importance.

No.	County.	Name of Place.	Remarks.
1	Antrim,	[illegible]	[illegible]
2	"	Ballycastle,	Opposite Rathlin Island.
3	Clare,	[illegible]	[illegible] Bay.
4	"	[illegible]	River Shannon.
5	"	[illegible]	[illegible] Bay, in [illegible] Bay.
6	"	[illegible]	[illegible]
7	"	[illegible]	South of Mal Bay.
8	"	[illegible]	[illegible] Bay and [illegible] Bay.
9	"	[illegible]	[illegible] Bay, at Mouth of Shannon.
10	"	[illegible]	[illegible] miles north-east of Black Head.
11	"	[illegible]	In River Shannon, off Kilrush.
12	"	[illegible]	[illegible] Bay.
13	"	[illegible]	Between [illegible] Bay and [illegible] Bay.
14	"	[illegible]	[illegible] Bay, at Mouth of Shannon.
15	"	[illegible]	About [illegible] miles north-east of Loop Head.
16	"	[illegible]	Opposite [illegible] Point, at south side of Galway Bay.
17	"	[illegible]	[illegible] of Miltown Malbay.
18	"	[illegible]	River Shannon, [illegible] miles east of Loop Head.
19	"	[illegible]	About [illegible] miles north-east of Loop Head.
20	"	[illegible]	About [illegible] miles north-east of Loop Head.
21	"	[illegible]	[illegible] Bay, [illegible] Point.
22	"	Kilrush,	River Shannon.
23	Cork,	[illegible]	[illegible] to Cork Harbour.
24	"	[illegible] Harbour,	[illegible] miles east of [illegible].
25	"	[illegible]	[illegible] of Cork Harbour.
26	"	[illegible]	North of [illegible] Harbour.
27	"	[illegible]	North side of [illegible] Bay.
28	"	[illegible]	North side of [illegible] Bay.
29	"	[illegible]	South side of [illegible] Bay.
30	"	[illegible]	At head of [illegible] Bay.
31	"	[illegible]	South side of [illegible] Bay.
32	"	[illegible]	North side of Dunmanus Bay.
33	"	[illegible]	Between Three Castle Head and Mizen Head.
34	"	[illegible]	[illegible]
35	"	[illegible] Island,	[illegible] Bay.
36	"	[illegible]	[illegible] Bay.
37	"	[illegible]	[illegible] of Cape Clear.
38	"	[illegible]	[illegible] Bay, north-west of [illegible] Head.
39	"	[illegible]	South side of [illegible] Harbour.
40	"	[illegible], Cape Clear,	North-east side of Cape Clear Island.
41	"	[illegible]	North side of [illegible] Bay.
42	"	[illegible]	[illegible] Bay, between [illegible] Bay and [illegible] Bay.
43	"	[illegible]	[illegible] miles north of Cork.
44	"	[illegible]	[illegible] Bay.
45	"	[illegible]	South side of [illegible] Bay, near [illegible] Head.
46	"	[illegible]	Between [illegible] and [illegible], in [illegible] Bay.
47	"	[illegible]	North of [illegible] Head, in [illegible] Bay.
48	"	[illegible]	[illegible] Bay, between [illegible] and [illegible] Head.

No.	County	Name of Place	Situation
49	Cork,	[illegible]	Opposite Dursey Island.
50	„	Dursey Sound,	East side of Dursey Island.
51	„	[illegible]	Between Dursey Island and Ballydonegan Bay.
52	„	[illegible]	South-west side of Ballydonegan Bay.
53	„	[illegible]	South side of Ballydonegan Bay.
54	„	Ballydonegan,	[illegible] side of Ballydonegan Bay.
55	„	[illegible]	Between Ballydonegan Bay and Cod's Head.
56	„	[illegible]	South-east of Cod's Head.
57	„	[illegible]	Near Cod's Head.
58	„	[illegible]	East of Cod's Head.
59	„	[illegible]	South side of Bantry Bay.
60	„	[illegible]	Bantry Bay.
61	„	[illegible]	[illegible] Bay, [illegible] Turland Bay and Lough Hyne.
62	„	[illegible] Point,	North side of [illegible] Harbour.
63	„	[illegible]	In River [illegible]
64	„	[illegible]	[illegible] Cod's Head.
65	„	[illegible]	[illegible] Bay.
66	Donegal,	[illegible]	Donegal Bay.
67	„	[illegible]	[illegible] Bay; in Donegal Bay.
68	„	[illegible]	Northern [illegible] of County Donegal.
69	„	Donegal,	At head of Donegal Bay.
70	„	[illegible]	[illegible] St. John's Point, Donegal Bay.
71	„	[illegible]	[illegible]
72	„	[illegible]	Between [illegible]
73	„	[illegible]	West shore of Lough Swilly.
74	„	[illegible]	[illegible] Bay, Lough Swilly.
75	„	[illegible]	West shore of Lough Swilly.
76	„	[illegible]	North of the [illegible]
77	„	[illegible]	East shore of Donegal Bay.
78	„	[illegible]	[illegible] St. John's Point, in Donegal Bay.
79	„	[illegible]	[illegible] Bay, in Donegal Bay.
80	„	[illegible]	[illegible] Bay.
81	„	[illegible] Island,	[illegible] of Donegal.
82	„	[illegible]	Between Lough Swilly and [illegible] Bay.
83	„	[illegible]	North-west side of Lough Foyle.
84	„	[illegible]	[illegible] in Donegal Bay.
85	„	[illegible]	Opposite [illegible] Point, Lough Foyle.
86	„	[illegible]	[illegible] Bay, between [illegible] Bay and Arran Island.
87	„	[illegible]	South of [illegible] Island, opposite Cruit Island.
88	„	[illegible] Island,	North of Cruit Island.
89	„	[illegible]	[illegible] Bay, in Donegal Bay.
90	„	[illegible]	[illegible] Bay, [illegible] Point.
91	„	[illegible]	[illegible] Bay.
92	„	[illegible]	[illegible] Bay, [illegible]
93	„	[illegible]	[illegible] of Dungloe.
94	„	Cruit Island,	[illegible] of the [illegible]
95	„	[illegible]	West side of [illegible]
96	„	[illegible]	South-west of [illegible]
97	„	[illegible]	South side of [illegible] Island.
98	„	[illegible]	Inner Bay in Donegal Bay.
99	„	[illegible]	East side of Arran Island.
100	„	[illegible]	North of the [illegible]
101	„	[illegible]	West side of [illegible] Bay.
102	„	Gola Sound, or Magheragallon.	Opposite Gola Island.
103	„	[illegible]	Between St. John's Point and [illegible], in [illegible] Bay.
104	„	[illegible]	Opposite [illegible], on south side of [illegible] Bay.
105	„	[illegible]	Near [illegible] Head [illegible] on east side of Lough Swilly.
106	„	[illegible]	North of [illegible] Bay, in Lough Swilly.
107	„	[illegible]	Near Tory Island.
108	„	[illegible] Island,	[illegible] of [illegible] Island.
109	„	[illegible]	South of [illegible]
110	Down,	Killough,	South-west of Ardglass.
111	„	[illegible]	Between [illegible] Bay and Carlingford Lough.
112	„	[illegible]	Between [illegible] Bay and Carlingford Lough.
113	„	[illegible]	West of [illegible] Island.
114	„	Cloghy,	Cloghy Bay, [illegible] of North Rocks.
115	„	Newcastle,	[illegible] north of [illegible] Head, in Dundrum Bay.
116	„	Portavogie,	Between Ballywalter and Cloghy.
117	Dublin,	Rush,	North of Dublin 15 miles.

No.	County.	Name of Place.	Situation.
118	[illegible]	[illegible]	[illegible]
119	,,	[illegible]	At [illegible], opposite north part of [illegible] Island.
120	Galway,	[illegible]	Galway Bay, east of Galway.
121	,,	[illegible]	At [illegible] of [illegible] Bay, in [illegible] Bay.
122	,,	[illegible]	[illegible] Bay, [illegible] of [illegible] Bay.
123	,,	[illegible]	[illegible] Harbour.
124	,,	[illegible]	[illegible] Bay, [illegible] of [illegible] Bay.
125	,,	[illegible]	[illegible] Bay, on north side of Galway Bay.
126	,,	[illegible]	Galway Bay.
127	,,	[illegible]	Mouth of Galway Bay.
128	,,	[illegible]	[illegible] Bay.
129	,,	[illegible]	[illegible] Bay, on south-east side of Galway Bay.
130	,,	[illegible]	Between [illegible] Bay and [illegible] Bay.
131	,,	[illegible]	[illegible] Bay, west of [illegible] Harbour.
132	,,	[illegible]	[illegible] Bay, north-west part of Galway Bay.
133	,,	[illegible]	East side of [illegible] Bay.
134	,,	Cove of [illegible]	[illegible] Sound, on [illegible] in Mid Island of Arran.
135	,,	[illegible]	West side of Kilkieran Bay.
136	,,	[illegible] Island,	West of [illegible] Island.
137	,,	[illegible]	[illegible], west of [illegible] Bay.
138	,,	Ard West	[illegible] Island.
139	,,	[illegible]	West shore of [illegible] Bay.
140	,,	[illegible]	[illegible] of [illegible]
141	,,	[illegible]	North side of [illegible] Bay.
142	,,	[illegible]	At head of [illegible] Bay.
143	,,	[illegible]	[illegible], or [illegible] Arran Island.
144	,,	[illegible]	[illegible], or North Arran Island.
145	,,	[illegible]	[illegible], or South Arran Island.
146	,,	[illegible]	North of [illegible] Bay.
147	,,	[illegible]	[illegible] Bay, on south-east side of Galway Bay.
148	,,	[illegible]	West of [illegible] Bay.
149	,,	[illegible]	Between [illegible] Point and [illegible] Pier.
150	,,	[illegible]	[illegible] Bay, on north side of Galway Bay.
151	,,	[illegible]	Head of [illegible] Bay.
152	,,	[illegible]	At head of [illegible] Bay.
153	,,	[illegible]	Between [illegible] Island and [illegible] Bay.
154	,,	[illegible]	[illegible] of [illegible] Island.
155	,,	[illegible]	[illegible], or North Arran Island.
156	,,	[illegible]	Kilkieran Bay.
157	,,	[illegible]	Opposite [illegible] Harbour.
158	,,	[illegible]	[illegible] side of [illegible]
159	,,	[illegible]	West of [illegible] Harbour.
160	,,	[illegible]	At head of [illegible] Bay.
161	,,	[illegible] Island,	North-west of [illegible] Island, which is north-west of [illegible] Island.
162	,,	[illegible]	West of [illegible] Island.
163	,,	[illegible]	Between [illegible] Bay and [illegible]
164	,,	[illegible]	West side of [illegible] Bay.
165	,,	[illegible]	At entrance of [illegible] Harbour.
166	,,	[illegible]	West side of [illegible] Bay.
167	,,	[illegible]	Between [illegible]
168	,,	[illegible]	[illegible] Bay, at head of [illegible] Bay.
169	,,	[illegible]	West of [illegible] Bay.
170	,,	[illegible]	Between [illegible] Point and [illegible], in [illegible] Bay.
171	,,	[illegible]	[illegible] Bay.
172	,,	[illegible] or [illegible]	[illegible] Bay.
173	,,	[illegible]	North-east of [illegible], in South Arran Island.
174	,,	[illegible]	West of [illegible]
175	,,	[illegible]	[illegible]
176	Kerry,	[illegible]	North shore of [illegible] Bay.
177	,,	[illegible]	South shore of [illegible] Bay.
178	,,	[illegible]	North side of Valentia Island.
179	,,	[illegible]	[illegible] Bay, [illegible] of [illegible] Island.
180	,,	[illegible]	West side of [illegible] Bay.
181	,,	[illegible]	West side of [illegible] Bay.
182	,,	[illegible]	East side of [illegible] Harbour.
183	,,	[illegible]	[illegible] Island:
184	,,	White Strand,	,, ,, [illegible]
185	,,	[illegible]	,, ,, [illegible]
186	,,	[illegible]	,, ,, [illegible]
187	,,	[illegible]	,, ,, [illegible]
188	,,	[illegible]	North shore of [illegible] Bay.
189	,,	[illegible]	[illegible] Harbour, opposite [illegible]

No.	County.	Name of Place.	Situation.
190	Kerry,	Dingle,	Entrance of Dingle Harbour.
191	„	Smerwick ([illegible]),	West side of Smerwick Harbour.
192	„	Ballinaraunig,	South side of Smerwick Harbour.
193	„	[illegible],	Between Brandon Head and Ballydavid Head.
194	Limerick,	Ringmoylan,	River Shannon, 11 miles below Limerick.
195	„	Beagh Castle,	River Shannon, 5 miles west of Ringmoylan.
196	„	Glin,	River Shannon.
197	„	[illegible],	At Glin, River Shannon.
198	Londonderry,	Portstewart,	3 miles north-west from Portrush.
199	Louth,	Carlingford,	Carlingford Lough.
200	„	Blackrock,	Dundalk Bay.
201	„	Giles's Quay,	North side of Dundalk Bay.
202	„	Clogher Head,	9 miles north-east of Drogheda.
203	„	Drogheda,	North of Dublin, 27 miles.
204	Mayo,	Carrowmore,	South side of Clew Bay.
205	„	[illegible],	South side of Westport Bay.
206	„	Belmullet,	Blacksod and Broadhaven Bays.
207	„	Inishturk,	Between Clare Island and Inishbofin.
208	„	Killala,	Killala Bay.
209	„	Lacken,	Lacken Bay, to the north-west of Killala Bay.
210	„	Mulranny,	North side of Clew Bay.
211	„	Dooagh,	West coast of Achill Island.
212	„	[illegible],	North side of Clew Bay.
213	„	Bunnacurry,	East coast of Achill Island.
214	„	Keel,	West coast of Achill Island.
215	„	Inishlyre,	Westport Bay.
216	„	Dooega,	South-west coast of Achill Island.
217	„	[illegible],	South coast of Peninsula of Curraun, north-west of Clew Bay.
218	„	Tonragee,	North coast of Peninsula of Curraun.
219	„	Portacloy,	Opposite the Stags of Broadhaven.
220	„	Porturlin,	About 4 miles east of Portacloy.
221	„	Dugort,	North coast of Achill Island.
222	„	Dooyork,	Between Claggan Head and Doohooma Head.
223	„	Achill Sound Viaduct,	Across the narrowest part of Achill Sound.
224	„	Belderrig,	Belderrig Harbour, on north coast of Mayo.
225	„	[illegible],	Southward of Downpatrick Head.
226	„	[illegible],	On mainland, at south part of Achill Sound.
227	„	Killerduff,	Bunatrahir Bay, about 3 miles south-west of Downpatrick Head.
228	„	Kilcummin,	Near Kilcummin Head, in Killala Bay.
229	„	Achill Beg,	Between Achill Island and Clew Bay.
230	„	Darreen,	Achill Island, near south entrance of the Sound.
231	„	Cloghmore,	South part of Achill Sound.
232	„	Darby's Point,	Achill Island, at the narrowest part of the Sound.
233	„	[illegible],	On mainland, at narrowest part of Achill Sound.
234	„	[illegible],	South-east side of Newport Bay.
235	„	Lecanvey,	Between Old Head and Murrisk.
236	„	Portawally,	South Island of Inishkea, west of the Mullet.
237	„	[illegible],	Between Inishbiggle, Annagh Island, and the mainland.
238	„	Clare Island,	South-east coast of Clare Island, which lies west of Clew Bay.
239	„	Kill,	South coast of Clare Island.
240	„	Ballytoohy,	North coast of Clare Island.
241	„	Tullaghan,	Between Blacksod and Tullaghan Bays.
242	„	Tonatanvally,	North-east coast of Achill Island.
243	„	Inver,	East side of Broadhaven Bay.
244	„	Dooghbeg,	North side of Clew Bay.
245	„	Dooniver,	North-east coast of Achill Island.
246	Sligo,	[illegible],	East side of Killala Bay.
247	„	[illegible],	North-west shore of Ballysadare Bay.
248	„	Inishcrone,	East side of Killala Bay.
249	„	Easky,	East of Lenadoon Point.
250	„	Aughris,	Near Aughris Head in Sligo Bay.
251	„	[illegible],	South-west of Aughris Head.
252	„	Lenadoon,	North-east point of Killala Bay.
253	„	Rosses,	North-west of town of Sligo.
254	„	Inishmurray,	Island south-west of Donegal Bay.
255	Waterford,	Cheekpoint,	Waterford Harbour.
256	„	Ardmore,	Ardmore Bay, between Youghal and Dungarvan Harbours.
257	„	Hackett's Dock,	Passage East, Waterford Harbour.
258	„	Ballinagoul,	South shore of Dungarvan Harbour.
259	„	Cunnigar,	Across Dungarvan Harbour.
260	„	Boatstrand,	Dunabrattin Bay, west of Tramore Bay.

No.	County.	Name of Place.	Situation.
361	Waterford,	Tramore,	South of Waterford, 7 miles.
362	Wexford,	Ballyhack,	Waterford Harbour.
363	"	Kilmore,	East of Forlorn Point.
364	"	Rosslare,	On Promontory forming south-east boundary of Wexford Harbour.
365	"	Ingard Point,	Southwest point of Fethard Bay.
366	"	Bannow,	East of Bannow Bay.
367	Wicklow,	Greystones,	South of Bray, about 5 miles.
368	"	Bray,	South of Dublin, about 12 miles.

PIERS AND HARBOURS.

Out of the foregoing, acting as members of the Fishery Piers and Harbours Commission, appointed under the Act 46 & 47 Vict., c. 26, we have, after holding public enquiries, recommended the cases in the following list, which shows the amount allocated for each work, and the sources from which the amounts were to be made up.

No.	County.	Name	Estimate £ s. d.	Grant £ s. d.	Loan £ s. d.	Cash Contributions £ s. d.	Total £ s. d.
1	Antrim,	[illegible]	1,600 0 0	1,600 0 0	—	—	1,600 0 0
2	Clare,	Liscannor,	6,000 0 0	[illegible]	[illegible]	—	[illegible]
3	Do.	Seafield,	[illegible]	[illegible]	[illegible]	—	[illegible]
4	Do.	[illegible]	[illegible]	[illegible]	310 0 0	[illegible]	[illegible]
5	Do.	[illegible]	[illegible]	[illegible]	[illegible]	—	[illegible]
6	Cork,	[illegible]	[illegible]	[illegible]	—	—	[illegible]
7	Do.	[illegible]	[illegible]	[illegible]	—	—	[illegible]
8	Do.	Ross,	[illegible]	[illegible]	—	[illegible]	[illegible]
9	Do.	Union Hall,	[illegible]	[illegible]	—	[illegible]	[illegible]
10	Do.	Ballycotton,	[illegible]	[illegible]	[illegible]	[illegible]	[illegible]
11	Do.	Castletown Berehaven,	[illegible]	[illegible]	—	—	[illegible]
12	Donegal,	Malin Head,	[illegible]	[illegible]	[illegible]	[illegible]	[illegible]
13	Do.	[illegible]	[illegible]	[illegible]	[illegible]	[illegible]	[illegible]
14	Do.	Portsalon,	[illegible]	[illegible]	[illegible]	[illegible]	[illegible]
15	Do.	[illegible]	[illegible]	[illegible]	—	[illegible]	[illegible]
16	Do.	[illegible]	[illegible]	[illegible]	—	—	[illegible]
17	Do.	[illegible]	[illegible]	[illegible]	—	—	[illegible]
18	Down,	Annalong,	[illegible]	[illegible]	[illegible]	[illegible]	[illegible]
19	Do.	[illegible]	[illegible]	[illegible]	[illegible]	[illegible]	[illegible]
20	Do.	Ballywalter,	[illegible]	[illegible]	[illegible]	[illegible]	[illegible]
21	Dublin,	Loughshinny,	[illegible]	[illegible]	—	[illegible]	[illegible]
22	Galway,	[illegible]	[illegible]	[illegible]	—	—	[illegible]
23	Do.	[illegible]	[illegible]	[illegible]	—	—	[illegible]
24	Do.	Cleggan,	[illegible]	[illegible]	[illegible]	—	[illegible]
25	Do.	[illegible]	[illegible]	[illegible]	—	—	[illegible]
26	Do.	[illegible]	[illegible]	[illegible]	—	—	[illegible]
27	Do.	[illegible]	[illegible]	[illegible]	—	—	[illegible]
28	Do.	[illegible]	[illegible]	[illegible]	—	—	[illegible]
29	Do.	[illegible]	[illegible]	[illegible]	—	—	[illegible]
30	Do.	[illegible]	[illegible]	[illegible]	—	—	[illegible]
31	Do.	[illegible]	[illegible]	[illegible]	—	—	[illegible]
32	Do.	[illegible]	[illegible]	[illegible]	—	—	[illegible]
33	Do.	[illegible]	[illegible]	[illegible]	—	—	[illegible]
34	Do.	[illegible]	[illegible]	[illegible]	—	—	[illegible]
35	Kerry,	[illegible]	[illegible]	[illegible]	—	—	[illegible]
36	Do.	[illegible]	[illegible]	[illegible]	—	—	[illegible]
37	Do.	Ballydavid,	[illegible]	[illegible]	[illegible]	—	[illegible]
38	Do.	Dingle,	[illegible]	[illegible]	—	—	[illegible]
39	Limerick,	[illegible]	[illegible]	[illegible]	—	—	[illegible]
40	Londonderry,	Portstewart,	4,000 0 0	[illegible]	[illegible]	—	[illegible]
41	Louth,	Carlingford,	[illegible]	[illegible]	[illegible]	—	[illegible]
42	Do.	Clogher Head,	[illegible]	[illegible]	[illegible]	[illegible]	[illegible]
43	Mayo,	[illegible]	[illegible]	[illegible]	[illegible]	—	[illegible]
44	Do.	Belmullet East,	[illegible]	[illegible]	—	—	[illegible]
45	Do.	Belmullet West,	[illegible]	[illegible]	—	—	[illegible]
46	Do.	[illegible]	[illegible]	[illegible]	—	—	[illegible]
47	Do.	[illegible]	[illegible]	[illegible]	—	—	[illegible]
48	Do.	[illegible]	[illegible]	[illegible]	—	—	[illegible]
49	Do.	Darby's Point, Achill,	[illegible]	[illegible]	—	—	[illegible]
50	Do.	[illegible]	[illegible]	[illegible]	—	—	[illegible]
51	Sligo,	[illegible]	[illegible]	[illegible]	—	—	[illegible]
52	Do.	Easky,	[illegible]	[illegible]	—	—	[illegible]
53	Do.	Aughris,	2,000 0 0	2,000 0 0	—	—	[illegible]
54	Waterford,	Cheekpoint,	[illegible]	[illegible]	—	[illegible]	[illegible]
55	Do.	Passage East,	[illegible]	[illegible]	—	[illegible]	[illegible]
56	Do.	[illegible]	[illegible]	[illegible]	[illegible]	[illegible]	[illegible]
57	Do.	[illegible]	[illegible]	[illegible]	—	—	[illegible]
58	Wexford,	Kilmore,	[illegible]	[illegible]	[illegible]	—	[illegible]
59	Wicklow,	Greystones,	10,800 0 0	[illegible]	[illegible]	[illegible]	[illegible]
		Total,	[illegible] 0 0	[illegible] 0 0	[illegible] 0 0	[illegible] 11 6	[illegible] 18 6

The following is a Return of the Works recommended, with the amount of the estimates of the Engineer to the Board of Public Works, the amount of the contracts where contractors have been obtained by the Board, and the date for the completion of the Works:—

No.	County.	Name.	Estimate. £ s. d.	Contract. £ s. d.	Date to be completed.	Date completed.
1	Antrim,	[illegible]	1,900 0 0	900 0 0	1st June, 1887,	
2	Clare,	[illegible]	[illegible]	[illegible]	31st Oct., 1886,	
3	Do.,	[illegible]	[illegible]	[illegible]	1st Oct., 1885,	
4	Do.,	[illegible]	[illegible]	Day's labour.	—	
5	Do.,	Carrigaholt,	[illegible]	[illegible]	1st Nov., 1886,	Nov., 1886.
6	Cork,	[illegible]	[illegible]	[illegible]	1st Feb., 1886,	March, 1886.
7	Do.,	[illegible]	[illegible]	[illegible]	2nd Nov., 1885,	
8	Do.,	[illegible]	[illegible]	[illegible]	1st Mar., 1886,	
9	Do.,	[illegible]	[illegible]	[illegible]	[illegible]	
10	Do.,	[illegible]	[illegible]	[illegible]	[illegible]	
11	Do.,	[illegible]	[illegible]	[illegible]	[illegible]	
12	Donegal,	[illegible]	[illegible]	[illegible]	1st Oct., [illegible]	
13	Do.,	[illegible]	[illegible]	[illegible]	1st Nov., [illegible]	December, 1885.
14	Do.,	[illegible]	[illegible]	[illegible]	1st Oct., [illegible]	
15	Do.,	[illegible]	[illegible]	[illegible]	1st Dec., [illegible]	July, 1886.
16	Do.,	[illegible]	[illegible]	[illegible]	1st May, [illegible]	May, 1886.
17	Do.,	[illegible]	[illegible]	[illegible]	1st June, [illegible]	
18	Down,	[illegible]	[illegible]	[illegible]	1st Mar., [illegible]	
19	Do.,	[illegible]	[illegible]	[illegible]	1st Nov., [illegible]	
20	Do.,	[illegible]	[illegible]	[illegible]	1st Oct., 1887,	
21	Dublin,	[illegible]	[illegible]	[illegible]	...	
22	Galway,	[illegible]	[illegible]	Day's labour.	...	
23	Do.,	[illegible]	[illegible]	do.	...	
24	Do.,	[illegible]	[illegible]	[illegible]	1st Oct., [illegible]	
25	Do.,	[illegible]	[illegible]	Day's labour.	—	
26	Do.,	[illegible]	[illegible]	[illegible]	1st Oct., [illegible]	Now carried on by day's labour.
27	Do.,	[illegible]	[illegible]	Day's labour.	...	
28	Do.,	[illegible]	[illegible]	do.	...	
29	Do.,	[illegible]	[illegible]	do.	—	
30	Do.,	[illegible]	[illegible]	do.	...	
31	Do.,	[illegible]	[illegible]	do.	...	
32	Do.,	[illegible]	[illegible]	do.	...	May, 1886.
33	Do.,	[illegible]	[illegible]	do.	...	
34	Do.,	[illegible]	[illegible]	do.	—	
35	Kerry,	[illegible]	[illegible]	[illegible]	1st June, [illegible]	May, 1886.
36	Do.,	[illegible]	[illegible]	[illegible]	[illegible]	Now carried on by day's labour.
37	Do.,	[illegible]	[illegible]	Day's labour.	...	
38	Do.,	Dingle,	[illegible]	[illegible]	[illegible]	[illegible]
39	[illegible]	[illegible]	[illegible]	...	—	[illegible]
40	Londonderry,	[illegible]	[illegible]	[illegible]	1st Oct., [illegible]	
41	Louth,	[illegible]	[illegible]	[illegible]	1st Nov., [illegible]	
42	Do.,	[illegible]	[illegible]	[illegible]	1st Oct., [illegible]	
43	Mayo,	[illegible]	[illegible]	[illegible]	1st Oct., [illegible]	[illegible], 1886.
44	Do.,	[illegible]	[illegible]	Day's labour.	—	
45	Do.,	[illegible]	[illegible]	do.	...	
46	Do.,	[illegible]	[illegible]	[illegible]	[illegible]	
47	Do.,	[illegible]	[illegible]	Day's labour.	...	
48	Do.,	[illegible]	[illegible]	do.	—	
49	Do.,	[illegible]	[illegible]	[illegible]		
50	Do.,	[illegible]	[illegible]	[illegible]	[illegible]	Now carried on by day's labour.
51	Sligo,	[illegible]	[illegible]	[illegible]	1st Oct., [illegible]	
52	Do.,	[illegible]	[illegible]	[illegible]	1st Oct., [illegible]	
53	Do.,	[illegible]	[illegible]	[illegible]	1st [illegible]	[illegible], 1886.
54	Waterford,	[illegible]	[illegible]	[illegible]	1st [illegible]	
55	Do.,	[illegible]	[illegible]	[illegible]	1st [illegible]	
56	Do.,	[illegible]	[illegible]	[illegible]	1st Nov., [illegible]	July, 1886.
57	Do.,	[illegible]	[illegible]	[illegible]	1st Oct., [illegible]	May, [illegible]
58	Wexford,	[illegible]	[illegible]	[illegible]	1st [illegible]	
59	Wicklow,	[illegible]	[illegible]	[illegible]	1st [illegible]	

With respect to Works not completed within the time specified in Contracts, the following information has been furnished by the Board of Works.

No.	[illegible]	[illegible]	[illegible]	[illegible]
[illegible]	[illegible]	[illegible]	[illegible]	[illegible]

In addition to the sums allocated out of the £250,000 for the different counties by way of grants, or grants and loans, a sum of £7,939 14s. 6d. was provided by persons interested, as cash contributions in aid of works, in the following counties, in order to make up the amounts of the estimates for the works:—

Counties.	Cash Contributions.			Grants.			Loans.			Total Estimates for Works.		
	£	s.	d.	£	s.	d.	£	s.	d.	£	s.	d.
Clare,	110	0	0	19,100	0	0	5,080	0	0	24,300	0	0
Cork,	2,850	0	0	28,100	0	0	2,800	0	0	33,750	0	0
Donegal,	795	0	0	23,930	0	0	3,275	0	0	27,200	0	0
Down,	1,100	0	0	13,800	0	0	3,500	0	0	18,400	0	0
Dublin,	276	1	6	1,899	10	0	—			2,175	11	6
Louth,	250	0	0	24,000	0	0	7,750	0	0	32,000	0	0
Waterford,	1,828	10	0	12,913	10	0	174	0	0	14,915	0	0
Wicklow,	500	0	0	8,500	0	0	1,000	0	0	10,000	0	0
Total,	7,939	14	6	131,645	0	0	23,156	0	0	162,740	14	6

In the remaining counties there were no cash contributions, and the grants, or grants and loans, made for the works were :—

Counties.	Grants.			Loans.			Total Estimates.		
	£	s.	d.	£	s.	d.	£	s.	d.
Antrim,	1,000	0	0	—			1,000	0	0
Galway,	22,250	0	0	2,000	0	0	24,250	0	0
Kerry,	7,800	0	0	600	0	0	8,400	0	0
Limerick,	19	0	0	—			19	0	0
Londonderry,	3,000	0	0	1,000	0	0	4,000	0	0
Mayo,	16,780	0	0	250	0	0	17,030	0	0
Sligo,	12,000	0	0	—			12,000	0	0
Wexford,	6,375	0	0	2,125	0	0	8,500	0	0
Total,	69,224	0	0	5,975	0	0	75,199	0	0

	£	s.	d.	£	s.	d.
Total Estimates for Works recommended,				237,939	14	6
Provided for by Cash Contributions,	7,939	14	6			
" Grants,	200,869	0	0			
" Loans,	29,131	0	0			
				237,939	14	6
Amount reserved for Expenses as mentioned above,				20,000	0	0
Total,				257,939	14	6

SUMMARY

Allocation of Sea Fisheries Fund of £250,000 for Piers and Harbours, under Act 46 & 47 Vict., cap. 26.

	£	s.	d.
Amount recommended by Grants,	200,869	0	0
Amount recommended by Loans,	29,131	0	0
Amount reserved by Board of Works for Expenses,	20,000	0	0
Total Amount of Fund,	250,000	0	0

The Herring Fisheries.

By the returns which we have received the capture of herrings would appear to have been greater in 1885 than in the year 1884, the number of mease shown as captured being 107,679, whereas in 1884 the number was 103,393.

The prices realised at the different stations will be seen in the returns below.

Previous to 1876, the capture of herrings at Kinsale was so insignificant that returns of the quantity taken were not called for by this department, but since that year they have been regularly supplied.

In 1875 it was observed that towards the close of the mackerel season a few herrings of fine quality were taken in the nets fishing for mackerel. This induced the owners of a few boats to bring over their trains of herring nets on the following year, so as to commence herring fishing towards the end of the mackerel season, when the latter became very low in price, and was not remunerative.

The success of the experiment was so considerable that **it led to an increase of** herring boats attending the fishing along the southern coasts, **and it has now become** a really substantial fishery.

At first it was confined mainly to vessels attending the fishery from Kinsale, but as will be seen by reference to the following returns it is now prosecuted from various stations—from Baltimore, County Cork, to Dunmore East, County Waterford—the number of vessels employed in this fishery will be seen by reference to the return below.

It has only very recently been discovered that herrings in great numbers can be taken off Dungarvan Bay. In 1884 the fishing there was confined to a few vessels from Arklow. In 1885 the number of Irish boats increased to 11, and two Scotch. The fishing was so successful that in the ensuing season it is hoped the number will be very much increased, as the attention of the herring fishermen has been drawn to the success experienced in 1884 and 1885.

Herring Fishery, 1885.

—	Boats employed, and highest number on any One day				Total Quantity, No. of Mease	Average Price	Total Value
	English.	Scotch.	Irish.	Manx.			
						£ s. d.	£
Kinsale, between 1st June and 10th September,	2	480	30	1	8,874	1 19 1	[illegible]
[illegible]	–	–	[illegible]	–	6,068	0 10 1	[illegible]
[illegible]	2	[illegible]	[illegible]	4	[illegible]	0 7 [illegible]	[illegible]
[illegible]	–	[illegible]	[illegible]	–	[illegible]	1 1 [illegible]	[illegible]
[illegible]	6	[illegible]	[illegible]	[illegible]	[illegible]	0 19 [illegible]	[illegible]
[illegible]	–	–	[illegible]	[illegible]	[illegible]	[illegible]	[illegible]
[illegible]	[illegible]	14	[illegible]	[illegible]	[illegible]	[illegible]	[illegible]
[illegible]	[illegible]	[illegible]	[illegible]	–	[illegible]	0 18 [illegible]	[illegible]
[illegible]	–	–	13	–	[illegible]	[illegible]	[illegible]
[illegible]	–	[illegible]	[illegible]	[illegible]	[illegible]	[illegible]	[illegible]
[illegible]	–	[illegible]	[illegible]	–	[illegible]	[illegible]	[illegible]
[illegible]	–	[illegible]	[illegible]	[illegible]	[illegible]	[illegible]	[illegible]
[illegible]	[illegible]	[illegible]	[illegible]	12	[illegible]	[illegible]	[illegible]
[illegible]	–	[illegible]	[illegible]	–	[illegible]	[illegible]	[illegible]
[illegible]	–	–	190	–	[illegible]	[illegible]	[illegible]
[illegible]	–	–	–	–	[illegible]	[illegible]	[illegible]
Total,					107,679	0 14 [illegible]	[illegible]

In consequence of allegations that the herring fishing in the waters of the south coast commencing so early in April, seriously affected the mackerel and hake fishing, by destroying large quantities of immature fish, we held public meetings at Kinsale on 19th, and at Baltimore the 23rd June last, which were very numerously attended by fish buyers, boat owners, and fishermen.

The result of our inquiries satisfied us that throughout the month of April the herrings captured were of a very inferior quality, and of little value. Even in the month of May they sold for from 4s. to 6s. per mease—a very unremunerative price, but that about the beginning of June the prices realized rose to about £2 per mease.

We were of opinion that the practice of herring fishing so early in the season on the coast was detrimental to the fishery, and we recommended the fishermen not to commence operations in future until the beginning of June. This recommendation was conveyed through the Government to the Scotch Fishery Board, requesting their co-operation. That Board arranged to issue a circular to their officers to bring the facts represented by us before the owners of fishing vessels in their districts who are in the habit of prosecuting the herring fishing on the coast of Ireland.

It is hoped that this will have the desired effect, and that the fishing will not be commenced until after the 1st of June.

Under any circumstances, however, it is open to the fish buyers, by arrangement amongst themselves, to regulate the season, by notifying that they will not buy before a certain date.

It will be seen by referring to the foregoing table that a very considerable capture of herrings took place during the year in Donegal Bay, the fish being of very fine quality.

SUBSTANCE OF REPORTS FROM COASTGUARD DIVISIONS.

DUBLIN DIVISION.

From Howth to Greystones, both stations inclusive.

According to the Coast Guard returns, there are in this division 164 fishing craft, with 581 men, and 44 boys, as compared with 152 vessels, 534 men, and 85 boys, in 1864.

Trawling, long and hand lines, herring nets and draft nets, are the means of capture.

Herring, mackerel, cod, plaice, bass, [illegible], sole, turbot, and whiting are taken.

Lobsters, in very limited numbers, and crabs, were taken round Ireland's Eye.

The conduct of the fishermen was good.

No part of the division is unguarded.

Clearing out the harbour at Howth would be of great benefit to the fisheries, and it is anticipated that the works now in course of construction at Greystones (at an estimated cost of £10,000) upon the recommendation of the Piers and Harbours Commission, will prove of great use to [illegible] fishing off that part of the coast.

Considerable quantities of French and American oysters have been put down on the oyster beds at Sutton and Clontarf.

ARKLOW DIVISION.

From the Breaches, County Wicklow, 7½ miles north of Arklow, North, to the Sluices, 1½ miles south of Cahore Point, County Wexford, South, a length of [illegible] miles.

No portion of this division unguarded.

The Coastguard Returns show, as employed in the fisheries during 1865, 235 vessels, 1,086 men and 26 boys.

Of the boats, 6 were of the first-class, 165 second, and 62 of the third.

The fish principally taken are herrings, cod, conger, ling, oysters, and trawl fish. Mode of fishing—nets, lines, dredges, and trawls.

The fishermen are reported to have been orderly and well conducted—no conflicts have taken place amongst them.

The Inspecting Commander reports, that the new pier at Wicklow affords good shelter for fishing boats except in N.E. winds—and that at Arklow, the new pier although not completed has "lowered the Bar so that fishing boats can enter at nearly all tides, whereas they had to wait for tide, and be dragged over the bar at times."

WEXFORD DIVISION.

From the Sluices, 1½ miles south of Cahore Point, to Bannow Bay, 54 miles.

The Harbour of Wexford, from Rosslare to Raven point, is unguarded, being under the control of the Customs authorities.

In this division there are 146 boats, 597 men, and 5 boys, engaged in sea-fishing. Of these 7 are first-class boats, 134 second, and 5 third.

Solely engaged in fishing, 29 boats, and 97 men; partially 117 boats, 480 men, and 5 boys. Fish generally captured—Herrings, mackerel, cod, bream, conger, gurnard, pollock, lobsters, and crabs.

Mode of fishing—hand lines and draft nets.

The following remarks are by the Inspecting Commander of the Coastguard, under date January 2nd, 1866:—

"During the past year the fisheries of this division have not been, I think, as productive as usual, owing to the rather unsettled and heavy weather that has prevailed more or less during the year.

At Morris Castle and Cahore, the boats launch from an open beach which, any thing of a breeze, [illegible] line of breakers, therefore except in perfectly fine weather no fishing is done, and at Cahore certainly the fishing has been poor.

At Rosslare the [illegible] fishing [illegible] weather, and I [illegible] South Bay [illegible] this last year.

At Carnsore the fishing [illegible] time [illegible] fishing [illegible] now. This should be one of the best fishing grounds [illegible] of fish [illegible]; I think that by

[illegible]

It is a great pity that a fishing harbour cannot be constructed … [illegible] … who pursue their calling all the year round."

Waterford Division.

From the East Bank of Barrow Ferry to Ballyvoile Head, north of Dungarvan Harbour.

This division extends along the coast for a distance of 63½ miles, all of which is guarded; but in the estuaries the following portions are unguarded:

From Oyster Point to Wellington Bridge, 5 miles; from Ballyhack to Fisherstown, 8 miles; from Glass House to Rockentown, 7 miles; from Cheekpoint to Blackrock, 16 miles; total 36 miles.

In the division there are 173 boats, 532 men, and 15 boys, employed in the sea fisheries; of these 10 are first class boats, 136 second class, and 27 third class.

Of the above there are solely engaged in fishing, 82 boats, 391 men, and 13 boys; partially so engaged, 90 boats and 241 men.

The fish principally captured are, mackerel, herrings, [illegible], whiting, bream, and soles, sprats, turbot, brill, plaice, hake, ling, and oysters. Sprats and mackerel are also taken in the largest quantities.

Mode of fishing.—hand lines, and a few trawlers.

No conflicts have occurred amongst the fishing population. The conduct of the fishermen has been uniformly reported as good.

Youghal Division.

From Ballyvoile Head, near Dungarvan, to Ballycotton; a distance of 36¼ miles.

Unguarded:—From Tallacoart Point to Ballyvoile Bridge, two miles; from Mine Head, East, to Gorrin River West, six and three quarter miles; from Capel Island to Ferry Point, five miles; from Glanyllam to Ballyeriveen, five miles; total, 18¾ miles.

By the Coastguard returns there were 39 boats and 224 men engaged exclusively in sea fishing; and 68 boats, 313 men, and 2 boys partially so engaged.

Of those solely engaged 7 of the boats were first class, 22 of the second, and 10 of the third.

Partially engaged, 1 of the first class, 42 of the second class, and 25 of the third class.

Mode of fishing.—Hand lines and long lines, trammel, drift, and draft nets.

A considerable herring fishery took place in Dungarvan Bay, and there is every prospect of its being further developed in the future, a large number of Arklow boats and some from Scotland attended the fishery and were fairly successful. It is expected that a large number of boats will attend during the coming season.

The following observations are from the report of the Divisional Officer of Coastguard:—

"*Ballinacourty.*—Difficulties in the way of landing the fish during the herring season, owing to the pier being inaccessible to the herring boats excepting at high water [illegible]. I am given to understand that railway accommodation is often deficient, many trains being left behind.

Helvick Head.—Difficulties in the way of landing at Ballinagoul, the pier there being only accessible at [illegible].

Ardmore.—Here also, the want of a suitable pier is felt, to enable a large class of boats to be used.

Knockadoon.—The pier recently erected at Knockadoon Head is found useful."

Queenstown Division.

From Garryvoe, in Ballycotton Bay, West, to Lane's Cottages, Ringabella Point, 3½ miles south of Queenstown, East.

Unguarded portion of Division.—All the estuary of Cork Harbour, from and including Queenstown, to the City of Cork.

The returns show that 186 boats, 560 men, and 18 boys were engaged in the sea fisheries in 1883, viz., 8 first class boats, 100 second class, and 78 third class. Of these 74 boats, 347 men, and 12 boys were solely engaged in fishing, and 112 boats, 213 men, and 6 boys partially so engaged.

The fishing is by means of trawls, long lines, hand lines, and seines.

No conflicts have occurred amongst the fishermen, who are reported to have been very orderly, sober, and industrious.

The following is from the report of the Divisional Officer of Coastguard :—

"The fisheries on the whole have been better in this Division than for the last two years—there have been good takes of hake and during August there were large shoals of mackerel in the harbour, but the only means of catching them were by rod and line.

Although the fishing last year was better than the two previous ones, all seem to agree in saying that it is not so good as formerly, and the general reason given is the discharge of the sand dredged up in the upper harbour outside.

The pier at Ballycottin is making good progress and will no doubt when finished be of great assistance to the fishermen of that place, by enabling them to employ larger boats, &c."

Kinsale Division.

From Myrtleville Point, 11 miles north-east of Kinsale East, to Galley Head; a distance of 110 miles.

In 1885 there were 218 boats, 993 men, and 56 boys reported to have been engaged in the sea fisheries; of these 47 boats, 282 men, and 40 boys were solely engaged in fishing, and 171 boats, 716 men, and 16 boys as only partially engaged.

The Inspecting Commander of Coastguard reports :—

"That the mackerel fishing for 1885, was not so good as previous years, perhaps owing to the cold weather experienced in spring."

Hake has been taken in large quantities, and the Inspecting Commander of Coastguard reports that the fishery is progressing.

Skibbereen Division.

From Galley Head to Snave Bridge, 21 miles east of Castletown Bere—about 170 miles.

Unguarded about 70 miles.

The returns from Coastguard show that in 1885 there were 396 boats, 1,680 men, and 14 boys employed in sea fisheries; of these, 108 boats, 592 men, and 9 boys, were solely engaged in fishing; and 288 boats, 1,088 men, and 5 boys, partially engaged.

Fish generally taken are cod, ling, mackerel, hake, pollock, bream, scad, and pilchards.

Modes of fishing—seines, hand and long lines, trawls, drift nets, and trammels.

The following is the Report of the Divisional Officer :—

"The fishing during the past year has been I consider on the whole successful—for while there were not such large quantities of mackerel taken as has been the case in some former years, this deficiency was, in my opinion, amply compensated by the takes of herrings, hake, and sprats. The herring fishing is in this division a new branch of industry, and was, I regret to say, not much availed of by the local first-class boats in consequence of their not having herring trains as a rule, but this want will, I hope, be non-existent next season, if sufficient necessary assistance can be granted on loan for the purchase of herring trains. The herrings in the latter end of June and during July were very fine, and in excellent condition, averaging one pound per mease of five hundred. The Scotch boats did almost all this fishing, and as there are plenty of fish and open water there is room for a large increase of boats prosecuting this class of fishing, which I hope will be supplied by the local boats obtaining herring trains. On one occasion £600 worth of herrings were purchased in one morning in Castletownsend Harbour alone. Hake has been very plentiful at times—I heard of several boats on one occasion averaging as much as forty fish per man for the night's fishing, price about 6d. per fish. There is a considerable increase in the trawling industry, several Cork boats, and I am glad to say several boats from Union Hall and Castletownsend, having been busily at work on the trawling grounds in this neighbourhood. Buyers have been established at several places and in consequence the price of fish has risen considerably. Turbot which used to be 3d. per lb. is now 1s. per lb., brill and sole, for which previously there was no regular sale, command 6d. per lb.; lobsters fairly plentiful, crabs not valued much and only sold locally, no pilchards that I am aware of, bream, gurnard both red and black, and pollock fairly plentiful. I would recommend as much assistance as possible be given to fishermen for the purpose of providing themselves with suitable and good gear for the capture of the vast quantities of fish which frequent this coast. Dunmanus Bay almost always has fish of some sort or description shoaling in it, but from its natural conformation, and from the poverty of the fishermen on its shores, nothing like an adequate capture is made."

No conflicts have occurred amongst the fishermen, who are reported as very orderly.

Castletown Division.

From Kenmare Bridge to Snave Bridge, 21 miles east of Castletown Bere, Bantry Bay.

A considerable portion of the coast in this division is unguarded, viz. :—From Bank-cove to Snave Bridge; Ardgroom to Kenmare, 26 miles; Ballydonegan to Dursey, 9 miles.

The returns show that in 1885 there were 160 boats, 834 men, and 77 boys, partially engaged in the sea fisheries.

The fish in general frequenting the coast are mackerel, pilchards, herrings, cod, ling, hake, pollock, whiting, &c.

Modes of capture—seines, herring nets, long lines, and hand lines.

Lobsters are captured in fair quantities.

The following remarks are by the Divisional Officer of Coastguard :—

"The great desiderata for the development of the fisheries in this division seem to me to be the question of a suitable pier at Castlecove, and some sort of shelter for the boats employed to the north, especially at Ballydonegan—where there is absolutely no protection whatever—and where the largest quantities are captured by the local boats nearly all the year round. Large shoals of sprat have made their appearance on the coast (a sure index of a good fishing season), the result of which is immediately seen in the capture of hake, some boats catching as much as 600 at once in their trammels. I am glad to be able to report that the haddock, which have practically deserted the coast for the last thirty years, have again made their appearance.

"No conflicts amongst the fishermen, who are reported as being most orderly and quiet."

Valentia Division.

From Kenmare Bridge, South, to Inch Point, 14 miles east of Dingle, North.

Length of coast line, 170 miles. Unguarded, 54 miles, viz.:—Inch to Rossbeigh, 40 miles; Rossbeigh to Carter's Cove, 9 miles; Bray Head to Bramble Point, including Beginnis Island, 5 miles.

By the Coastguard returns there were 153 boats, 804 men, and 6 boys, engaged in the sea fisheries, viz.:—Solely engaged in fishing, 4 boats and 10 men; partially engaged, 150 boats, 794 men, and 6 boys.

The kinds of fish generally captured are—turbot, soles, bream, brit, plaice, gurnard, cod, ling, hake, conger, pollock, scad, mackerel, haddock, pilchards, &c.

The Coastguard report is as follows :—

"The sea fishing off the coast of this division has not been so very good this season—Ballinskelligs being the worst for many years—the fish not coming so close in shore as formerly, and no boats large enough to go out into deep water with safety, and the seines cannot take in deep water. At times the fish were plentiful off the coast, but there were not adequate means for their capture.

"There have been no conflicts amongst the fishermen, who are reported as being very orderly."

Dingle Division.

From Inch Point, 14 miles east of Dingle, South, to Blennerville, 2 miles south-west of Tralee North; length, 80 miles.

Unguarded, viz.:—Tower Clove to Clogher Head, including the Blasket Islands, 8 miles; Brandon Creek to Blennerville Bridge, including Maharee Islands, 40 miles; total, 48 miles.

The returns from the Coastguard for 1885, show there were 171 boats, 573 men, and 11 boys engaged in the sea fisheries, viz.:—solely engaged in fishing, 66 boats, 208 men, and 11 boys; partially engaged, 105 boats and 365 men.

Herrings, mackerel, soles, turbot, brill, ling, cod, hake, pollock, bream, whiting, gurnard, abound along this coast.

The Divisional Officer of Coastguard reports as follows :—

1. "The fishing in this division for the past twelve months has been very good. The mackerel last year was not quite so good as in 1884. Trawling very good in Dingle Bay, and outside a few herrings. The fishermen complain very much as to the want of a light at the mouth of the harbour, as they frequently have to lie in the bay all night when coming in late. They also complain of the shallowness of the water in mid-channel, which is caused by a sand bank, which, if removed, and a light fixed at the entrance of the harbour, would be a great boon to the fishermen, and further the fishing interests in the locality.

2nd. "The road leading from Murreagh to Ballydavid Coastguard Station, where they are about to erect a slip and breakwater, is in a very bad condition—scarcely room enough for a cart to pass to and fro with the fish that is brought from the boats, and as the sea is encroaching, I am certain that in a few more months a cart will not be able to pass—in fact it is not safe at present—a new road is very much required. Should an accident occur on the road there is nothing whatever to keep the occupants and car from falling on the rocks below; by this road fish is brought to the local markets. The moneys advanced on reproductive loans and the relief nets have benefited the men very much.

"No conflicts amongst the fishing population—the fishermen being reported as very orderly.

N.B.—"The Fishery Piers and Harbour Commissioners have recommended an expenditure of £800 to provide a light at the entrance of Dingle Harbour."

BALLYBUNION DIVISION.

From Blennerville, county Kerry, to Foynes.

In this division there are 85 boats registered, employing [illegible] men and 17 boys. They are divided into 1 first-class, employing 7 men, and 7 second-class, employing 18 men, solely engaged; and 8 second-class with 32 men, and 69 third-class with [illegible] men, only partially engaged in fishing. This shows a decrease of 17 boats in this year. The modes of fishing are nets and lines—no trawlers. Boats and gear are quite unsuitable for this coast, and the people are too poor to provide better. Shoals of mackerel and herring were seen off the coast in spring and harvest about half to one mile off the shore. Mackerel is taken in the largest quantities. Great quantities of herrings also appeared from latter part of August to December in Shannon, but the fishermen were not provided with proper nets.

The oyster beds in Tralee Bay and the Shannon are said to be improving, and more spatting this year than for the last ten years.

The fishermen are orderly and peaceable. No conflicts.

The Coast Guard Officer reports that there is an abundance of fish of all descriptions on this part of the coast as well as in the river. Lobsters and pollock innumerable along the rocks and often caught without a boat in the summer season, and a few miles off the land shoals of mackerel and herring of very large size. The people are, however, devoid of capturing them and understand but little about sea-fishing or management of boats. A great drawback is the want of piers and landing-places to secure boats in bad weather. [illegible]. Notwithstanding their primitive mode of fishing they sometimes make good captures, one boat having cleared £40 this year by lobsters alone, and this was only a small boat of 14 feet. A few piers and landing-places would stimulate to get boats and gear. Fenit harbour being now well advanced for the shelter and safety of boats would be likely to be a very good fishing station for all sorts of fishing vessels, being within a reasonable distance of deep sea-fishing grounds for mackerel and herring, and having a railway available for conveyance of fish to market.

SEAFIELD DIVISION, COUNTY CLARE.

From Ballymacrinan to Carracapple Head.

In this division there are 222 boats registered, employing 557 men and 8 boys. They are divided into the following, viz.:—Four second-class with 12 men, and 32 third-class boats with 87 men, solely engaged in fishing; and 186 third-class, with 449 men only partially so. There is an increase in the number of boats registered in this division of 14, and in the number of fishermen of 53.

The Coast Guard Officer reports that the fishing this year has been, on the whole, below the average, principally on account of bad weather.

The Coast Guard Officer reports that the new fishing pier at Carrigaholt, when completed, will not be able to afford shelter to any vessels of greater draught than 5 feet. Only a few vessels of that draught can find shelter under the lee of the pier during bad weather at low water.

Shoals of mackerel and herring appeared during August and up to December off part of the coast about one mile from the shore.

Oyster fisheries not improving. The fishermen are peaceable and orderly. No conflicts. Some of them complained of the stake nets injuring their fishing.

trawlers for injury to the lines of fishermen on the coast, and serious disputes have arisen on the subject. With this exception there have been no conflicts; the fishermen are reported as peaceable and orderly. Oyster fisheries not improving.

CLIFDEN DIVISION.

From Mason Island to Doaghbeg.

In this division there are 453 boats registered, employing 2,485 men and 1 boy. This is an increase of 38 boats and 132 men registered during the year. These are divided into 4 second-class, with 24 men, and 61 third-class with 271 men, solely engaged in fishing; and 221 second-class, with 894 men, and 166 third-class, with 1,296 men, only partially so. The fisheries in this division are much as usual—fish tolerably abundant, but the means of catching them inadequate, and no market for them when taken to encourage many more to follow fishing as a livelihood. Nets and lines are the modes of fishing—no trawling.

About 5,000 dozen have been taken during the past year. Mackerel appeared in great shoals from August to November off different parts of the coast, but the means of capture were inadequate. The difficulties of getting to market at any reasonable rate prevent the fisheries from being developed. If the railway from Clifden to Galway were completed it would tend to promote the fisheries materially. In many places along this coast the fishermen labour also under all the disadvantages attendant upon the want of proper harbours, in which boats suitable for the fishing could be kept.

The public oyster beds not improving, and only a small quantity of oysters brought to the private beds during the year. The fishermen are peaceable and orderly—no conflicts.

KEEL DIVISION.

From Doaghbeg to Fahy Head in Blacksod Bay.

In this division there are registered 72 boats, employing 253 men and 13 boys. They are divided into 1 second-class, with 2 men, and 71 third-class, with 251 men, only partially engaged in fishing.

The Coast Guard reports that mackerel in considerable abundance appeared off the coast about three miles off the land close in shore in July and August and as many as 217,000 were thus captured—principally at Keem Bay. Herring also appeared but not in such numbers as the mackerel, and about 120,000 were captured. About 45 tons of cod were killed principally between Clare Island and Achilbeg, and about 5,000 ling.

The season proved more successful than 1884; and if the younger portion of the fishing population remained at home a very large capture of fish might be made, even with their curraghs and imperfect gear. Piers or landing-places are much needed at Dugh.

The modes of fishing are nets and lines. The public oyster fisheries have not improved, nor have the private oyster layings been properly cultivated.

The fishermen are peaceable and orderly in their conduct.

BELMULLET DIVISION.

From Doona Head to Brandy Point.

In this division there are 143 boats registered, employing 593 men and 53 boys. They are all only partially engaged in fishing. The number has again decreased.

Nets and lines are the modes of fishing principally used. Large shoals of herring and mackerel appeared off parts of the coast from 500 yards to 3 miles off shore from August, and some in July to December. The means of capture were inadequate. The oyster fisheries have not improved.

The fishermen are peaceable and orderly.

The Coastguard officer reports that in his opinion the fisheries are in a backward state owing to the want of capital to procure larger boats and nets, and also that the people do not regard fishing as their chief calling. It seems, he thinks, to be the general opinion that the fish do not frequent this part of the coast in such numbers as formerly.

Ballycastle Division.

From Brandy Point to Gap of Barnagh.

In this division there are registered 133 boats, employing 644 men. They are divided into 4 second-class with 24 men, and 129 third-class with 620 men only partially engaged in fishing. The Coast Guard Officer reports that there being no regular fishermen in this division it is impossible to give an accurate idea of the state of the Fisheries. Large shoals of mackerel and herring have been seen off the coast and usually appear in February and August, and a few good takes have been made, but the boats being all small rowing boats the men only venture out in fine weather as there are no harbours for them to run into for shelter if it came on to blow suddenly.

Boat slips are being built at Ballycastle and Polnamuck, near Downpatrick Head, and the pier at Lacken is being lengthened. These will be a great convenience to the fishermen and tend to develop the fisheries. Nets and lines are the modes of fishing practised—no trawlers—but the fishermen cannot afford to buy fishing gear when most wanted and in consequence miss many opportunities. Large shoals of herrings and mackerel appeared off parts of the coast from May to October, from half to two and a half miles off shore, but there were not sufficient means for their capture. The fishermen require larger boats and landing places suitable to the requirements of such and improved modes of fishing. Lobsters are captured in large quantities in parts of the division.

The fishermen are peaceable and orderly.

Pullendiva Division.

From Ballina Quay to Coney's Island, Sligo.

There are registered in this division 47 boats, employing 208 men and 10 boys. They are divided into 4 second-class with 10 men and 6 third-class with 15 men, solely engaged in fishing; and 37 third class with 198 men only partially so.

The Coast Guard Officer reports that he considers there is plenty of fish along this coast, but the fishermen have not proper gear for their capture, nor the means to provide it.

The modes of fishing are nets and lines, trawling and lobster-pots. Trawling has increased, and there is good trawling ground off parts of the coast. Large shoals of herrings and mackerel appeared from September to middle of December from two to three miles off the shore, but no adequate means for capture. If the fishermen had proper harbours and good gear they could take a far greater quantity of fish. Lobsters were taken in large quantities. Oyster fisheries not improved. The fishermen are peaceable and orderly.

Sligo Division.

From Coney's Island to Donegal.

There are registered in this division 143 boats, employing 578 men and 19 boys. They are divided into 1 first-class with 4 men, 4 second-class with 10 men, and 5 third-class with 25 men solely engaged in fishing; and 13 second-class with 46 men, and 121 third-class with 492 men only partially so.

The Coast Guard Officer reports that the numbers of boats and hands engaged appears to be falling off considerably, chiefly, it is believed, owing to the poverty of all classes. Large quantities of herrings and mackerel appeared in Donegal Bay from August to October. Further seaward the shoals were much smaller, and remained only for a short time; on the whole, the catch was a very fair one. Lobsters have been caught in tolerable quantities. Trawlers are few and only appear to work from July to September. The fishermen have not suitable boats or gear to follow the fishing in deep water, and they are too poor to supply themselves with better. They are peaceable and orderly. No conflicts. The oyster fisheries are not improved.

Killybegs Division.

From Donegal Quay to Lower Ferry (Gweebarra River), Donegal.

There were in 1885, 150 boats, 807 men, and 24 boys, as compared with 177 boats, 845 men, and 17 boys, in 1884.

The modes of capture are nets, long lines, and hand lines.

The Coast Guard officer reports that white fish were very scarce this year, although some trawlers from Liverpool had good fishing in Donegal Bay, but on account of the weather had to leave before the season expired. It is stated that these vessels will again visit this part of the coast during the season of 1886, and will employ the local fishermen. It is to be hoped that this may be carried into effect, as it would be of importance to the people, both as giving employment and also instructing them in an improved mode of fishing. It is believed that the erection of the boat slip and breakwater at Malinmore, at an estimated cost of £1,500 on the recommendation of the Piers and Harbours Commission, will be of considerable benefit to the fishermen of the locality.

The fishermen were orderly and quiet.

GWEEDORE DIVISION.

From Gweebarra Bar to Oldcastle Point.

There were in 1885, 153 boats, 568 men, and 37 boys, as compared with 131 boats, 462 men, and 45 boys in 1884.

The modes of capture are seine nets, hand lines, and long lines.

The fish chiefly taken off this division are salmon, plaice, turbot, gurnet, cod, and large quantities of lobsters and crabs.

The fishing industry is not prosecuted with much energy in this division; it is chiefly confined to lobster and crab fishing. The great difficulty of transit to market, sometimes thirty to forty miles, or forty-five miles by sea, and the attendant expenses, are such as to give but small return for the labour, risk, and wear and tear of boats and gear, and gives the men but little encouragement to persevere.

The Divisional Officer of Coast Guard reports that a pier inside Gola Island on the mainland, where a steamer could call alongside and embark the fish, would be a great benefit to the fisheries, by inducing the employment of a larger class of boats to work the fishing grounds twenty or thirty miles off the coast. These grounds reported to be well stocked, are not worked at present.

The fishermen on this division were orderly and quiet.

RATHMULLAN DIVISION.

From Lough Swilly to Bloody Foreland.

There were in this division, in 1885, 215 boats, 806 men, and 90 boys, as compared with 213 boats, 815 men, and 97 boys in 1884.

The modes of capture were hand and long lines.

The principal capture consists of cod, herring, mackerel, haddock, whiting, flukes, turbot, sole, and plaice. There was also a large quantity of lobsters and crabs taken.

Large shoals of herrings were observed off the Sheephaven portion of the Division during January, August, and September, but no adequate means existed for their capture. On the whole 1885 was about an average year, as regards the fisheries of this division.

It is hoped that the pier and quay which is in course of construction at Portsalon, will have the effect of further developing the local fisheries. The works are being carried out in accordance with a recommendation of the Fishery Piers and Harbours Commission, the estimated cost being £4,450, it is expected they will be completed by the latter part of next year.

The conduct of the fishermen was very orderly and quiet.

MOVILLE DIVISION.

From Dunaff to Magilligan Point, County Derry.

There were, in this division, in 1885, 297 boats, and 991 men, as compared with 280 boats, 943 men, and 33 boys, in 1884.

Hand lines and long lines are used.

Turbot, herring, cod, ling, plaice, and pollack were taken, and also large quantities of lobsters and crabs.

Two important harbour works are being constructed within the limits of this division, one, the erection of a quay, and removal of rocks at Malin Head, at an estimated cost of £10,000; the other, the construction of a pier at Culdaff, at an estimated cost of £4,000. Both of these works were undertaken upon the recommendation of the Piers and Harbours Commission, and grants from the Sea Fisheries Fund made for the purpose; and it is trusted they will prove of great benefit to the fishermen who follow their profession off this exposed part of the coast.

The fishermen in this division were orderly and quiet.

Ballycastle Division.

From Downhill, county Londonderry, to Jenny's Bridge, county Antrim.

In this division, in 1885, there were 82 boats, 307 men, and 13 boys, as compared with 88 boats, 176 men, and 27 boys in 1884.

Hand lines and long lines are the modes of capture.

The usual modes of fishing off the coasts of this division are by means of long and hand lines. Seine nets are used off Ballycastle and Torr occasionally, and small otter trawls are also used in Ballycastle Bay. Trawling, however, is not carried on to a large extent by vessels of any size, but English and Scotch fishing vessels sometimes visit Portrush for a short period in the summer.

The Divisional Officer of Coast Guard also reports that the fishermen appear to have been as energetic as possible of late in their vocation, especially off Ballintrae, where he observed boats outside in very rough weather. The late accident near the Giant's Causeway (in which four men lost their lives), was occasioned by this risk.

The fish taken are cod and ling; the take of soles is small and uncertain. Plaice are taken in moderate quantities—crabs and lobsters continue to be taken in large quantities. Considerable advantage it is expected will be derived by the fishermen by the construction of the pier at Portstewart, and the boat slip at Portrush, which were inquired into by the Fishery Piers and Harbours Commissioners, and for the construction of which grants were recommended to be made out of the Sea Fisheries (Ireland) Fund, with the approval of the Lords Commissioners of Her Majesty's Treasury.

Fishermen throughout the division were generally orderly.

Carrickfergus Division.

From Jenny's Bridge to Fort William Park, near Belfast.

There were in this division, in 1885, 50 boats, and 128 men, as compared with 56 boats and 128 men in 1884.

The modes of capture used off the coast of this division are seine nets, drift nets, long lines, and hand lines. There are also a few small trawlers in the Whitehead district.

The fish principally captured are soles, brill, plaice, cod, turbot, ray, pollock, and herrings, also conger eels.

The fisheries in this division are unimportant, and the Inspecting Commander of Coast Guard reports that in Belfast Lough the fish are getting scarce, and keep farther out to sea. This, he suggests, is caused either by the increased quantity of sewage poured into the lough, or the increased number of steamers passing up and down. The daily discharging of 400 tons of mud from the Belfast Harbour extension works off Whitehead no doubt causes a further diminution.

This officer also states that the loss of the pier at Portmuck, Island Magee, which was carried away by a gale of wind in 1884, is felt by the fishermen there, as landing from boats is much interfered with.

With one of my colleagues, Mr. Brady, I held a meeting at the Court House, Carrickfergus, on the 7th of August, pursuant to public notice, to inquire into the state of the mussel fisheries in Belfast Lough, but from the evidence it appeared that mussel fishing in this immediate locality was of little or no importance. We however, held a further inquiry on the same subject on the next day at the Court House, Hollywood, to which I shall allude in its proper place, viz., Donaghadee Division.

Donaghadee Division.

From Kinnegar to Newcastle Quay.

During 1885, 149 boats, 455 men, and 49 boys were employed, as compared with 145 boats, 461 men, and 42 boys in 1884. Hand lines, long lines, drift nets, and seine nets are the modes of capture.

The fish principally captured are cod, pollock, herrings, ling, and a few mackerel, mussels are also taken.

The fisheries off this division are of an unimportant character.

As before mentioned, Mr. Brady and I held a meeting at the Court House, Hollywood, county Down, on the 8th of August, pursuant to public notice, to inquire into the state of the mussel fisheries it being reported to us that they were being exhausted by over dredging. Considerable interest was manifested in the inquiry, and we received an amount of evidence on the subject of the decline which has taken place in this fishery. The Rev. Mr. O'Laverty, P.P., who took a great interest in the question, gave us some very interesting evidence on the point, as did also some of those engaged in picking mussels, and a shell-fish buyer in Belfast, and it was proved that very large quantities of mussels were exported to Scotland. The weight of evidence went to show that this as well as all kinds of fishing were on the decline in Belfast Lough. We, therefore, considered the subject of so much importance, that we announced our intention of holding a series of Inquiries during 1886, to investigate the question; due notice of which we undertook to give to all persons concerned, and to the general public, so as to secure full and sufficient evidence on the point.

The fishermen in this division were reported to be very orderly and quiet.

Strangford Division.

From Newcastle Quay to Sheepland Head.

In 1885, 95 boats, 190 men, and 10 boys were employed, as compared with 101 boats, 166 men, and 4 boys, in 1884.

Nets and hand lines are the modes of capture.

The fish principally taken are herring, cod, pollock, mackerel and some lobsters and crabs, but the fisheries off this division cannot be said to be of much importance.

Some large shoals of herring and mackerel appeared off the Killard guard, in month of July, and remained three or four weeks. Shoals of these fish also appeared off the Strangford guard between July and September, but not of any great size.

The fishermen were very orderly and quiet.

Newcastle Division.

From Sheepland Head to Riverfoot, Kilkeel.

During 1885, 105 boats, 499 men, and 28 boys were employed, as compared with 131 boats, 555 men, and 27 boys, in 1884.

Trammel nets, hand lines, and long lines are the means of capture.

The fish which are captured in largest quantities off this division are herrings, mackerel, haddock, whiting, ling, cod, and conger. Two very important fishing centres are situated in this division, viz., Ardglass and Annalong. At the former of these places a large fleet of fishing vessels of different nationalities assemble each year to carry on the herring fishery. In 1885 there were represented by 5 English, 241 Scotch, 84 Irish, and 4 Manx vessels, the estimated value of the capture being £7,459. The improvement of the harbour (which is a Royal one) by the Board of Public Works it is hoped will be of benefit to the fishermen. At Annalong there were 5 English, 4 Scotch, and 15 Irish vessels engaged at the herring fishery, and the estimated amount realized by the capture was £4,300. It is expected that the improvements to the harbour also at this latter place for which a grant from the Sea Fisheries Fund was recommended by the Piers and Harbours Commissioners, and which was supplemented by contributions from local sources will when completed prove of great advantage to the fishermen frequenting this coast.

The average price realized was considerably less than in 1884, the capture also being much less.

Drogheda Division.

From Riverfoot, Kilkeel, to Maiden Tower, Drogheda.

During 1885, [illegible] boats, [illegible] men, and 44 boys were employed, as compared with 285 boats, [illegible] men, and [illegible] boys in 1884.

The modes of capture are nets and long lines.

The principal capture off this division consists of herrings, mackerel, whiting, cod, plaice, sole, and hake.

On the whole, it is considered that the take of fish off the coast of this division has been less than in previous years. The Inspecting Commander of Coastguard reports that the trawlers off the mouth of the Boyne constantly come inside the prohibited limits, and that it seems impossible with the means at the disposal of the Coastguard to prevent it. The men from the Boyne Coastguard Station captured 2 trawls in December by going off in small fishing boats; but the fines inflicted were so small that they could have little or no deterrent effect.

It is anticipated that the important harbour works now in course of construction at Clogher Head, Carlingford, and Kilkeel, will be of great advantage in developing the fisheries, not only in their immediate vicinity, but along all this portion of the east coast.

These works have all been undertaken upon the recommendations of the Piers and Harbours Commissioners, who voted a grant out of the Sea Fisheries Fund in each case, this being supplemented by Grand Jury presentments and local contributions. The works at Carlingford consist of the construction of a pier, boat slip, and excavating a portion of existing harbour, at an estimated cost of £[illegible].

At Clogher Head a pier is being erected and excavations carried out, so as to give a fair depth of water at low tide. This, it is anticipated, will do much to encourage the use of a larger class of craft than have hitherto existed off this part of the coast. There are a large number of trawlers which frequent this coast, and it is believed that Clogher Head will become a very important fishing centre as English, Scotch, and Manx vessels frequent this locality as well as the Irish boats. Up to the present, owing to the want of harbour accommodation, trawlers could only work for the summer months, having no place to shelter in broken weather.

At Kilkeel it is proposed to extend the pier and basin and construct two boat slips, at an estimated cost of £7,400. This latter place is of considerable importance as regards the herring fishery, and is largely frequented by Scotch and Irish vessels. The greatest number of boats fishing on any one day in 1885 was 4 English, 11 Scotch, 28 Irish, and 9 Manx. The capture for the season, which extends from 1st of June to 1st of November, was 4,[illegible] crans, valued at £[illegible].

The fishermen were orderly and quiet.

Malahide Division.

From Laytown to Baldoyle.

There were in 1885, 66 boats, 279 men, and 16 boys employed, as compared with 69 boats, 336 men, and 21 boys in 1884.

The modes of capture are trawling, herring nets, long lines, and hand lines.

Large quantities of herring and some mackerel were taken off this part of the coast. Turbot, cod, ling, and plaice were also captured, as well as large quantities of lobsters and crabs.

In our capacity of Fishery Piers and Harbour Commissioners, we held an inquiry at Lough Shinny Coastguard Station, respecting an application for a grant in aid of the construction of a pier and landing slip at this place. The whole of the small village is inhabited by fishermen, who bear the highest character for industry, courage, and respectability. At present there is no place where they can come alongside in their boats. The lords of the soil, Sir Roger Palmer, Bart., and Mr. Ion Trant Hamilton, D.L., expressed their intention of contributing towards the cost of constructing the pier. An old pier existed very many years ago, but has long since been washed away. It is feared, however, that the funds at the disposal of the Commissioners are not sufficient to provide the accommodation sought for, as the undertaking is likely to prove an expensive one; but of its utility and the justness of the claims of the people for improved accommodation there can be but one opinion.

The conduct of the fishermen has been very orderly.

IRISH REPRODUCTIVE LOAN FUND.

MR. BRADY'S REPORT FOR THE COUNTIES OF LEITRIM, SLIGO, MAYO, GALWAY, CLARE, LIMERICK, AND PART OF KERRY.

COUNTY LEITRIM.

No applications were received during the year. The total amount issued for this county for the eleven years ending 31st December, 1885, was only £100.

There are no arrears.

The county has only a very small seaboard, and there is really only one fishing crew in it.

COUNTY SLIGO.

There were forty-three applications received from fifty-four persons for £1,197. Out of this there were twenty-eight loans recommended, amounting to £608. The amount actually issued was £577. Two of the loans, amounting to £25, were cancelled. The loans ranged from £8 to £150, the latter being for oyster cultivation.

By the return received from the Board of Works, the following instalments are stated to be in arrear up to 1st January, 1886:—

	£	s.	d.
In the case of 1 of the loans made in 1875, amounting to	9	1	3
" 1 " 1876, "	3	19	9
" 2 " 1877, "	23	7	0
" 2 " 1878, "	21	8	8
" 1 " 1879, "	1	6	7
" 1 " 1880, "	8	3	0
" 5 " 1881, "	15	16	1
" 1 " 1882, "	11	9	4
" 1 " 1883, "	1	18	6
" 1 " 1884, "	1	6	7
Total arrears,	£97	13	6

out of the sum of £4,024 lent, the interest on which amounted to £376 19s. 3d.

These arrears are made up as follows:—

	£	s.	d.
1 instalment due in 1877, amounting to	1	6	5
5 " 1878, "	9	11	1
5 " 1879, "	9	19	4
4 " 1880, "	8	7	11
6 " 1881, "	15	4	6
5 " 1882, "	6	5	11
2 " 1883, "	1	6	0
1 " 1884, "	5	17	11
16 " 1885, "	31	1	6
Total, 46 instalments, amounting to	£97	13	6

I have looked into the cases stated to be in arrear, and find that, with but few exceptions, the money could be recovered if proper legal steps were adopted.

The total sum issued in this county for the eleven years ending 31st December, 1885, was £4,024, and the amount repaid according to Board of Works return was £2,227 13s. 3d. The outstanding promissory notes not arrived at maturity amounted to £1,283 15s. 11d.

COUNTY MAYO.

There were 887 applications received from 483 persons amounting to £3,284 9s. Out of these, 314 loans were recommended to 384 persons to the amount of £2,416 10s. The sum of £2,364 10s. was issued. Four of the loans amounting to £52 were cancelled.

The loans ranged from £5 to £50.

The loans made in this county have proved to have been particularly useful to the poor fishermen, many of whom should have abandoned fishing without them.

By the return received from the Board of Works the following instalments appear to be in arrears:—

		£	s.	d.
In the case of 2 loans made in 1875, amounting to	. . .	6	5	0
" 3 " 1876, "	. . .	34	18	11
" 4 " 1877, "	. . .	27	0	5
" 6 " 1878, "	. . .	25	0	0
" 7 " 1879, "	. . .	45	3	6
" 18 " 1881, "	. . .	36	10	0
" 21 " 1882, "	. . .	75	18	11
" 7 " 1883, "	. . .	9	17	0
" 3 " 1884, "	. . .	3	1	1
" 8 " 1885, "	. . .	3	3	0
	Total arrears,	£283	19	10

out of a sum of £9,267 8s. lent, the interest on which amounted to £528 18s. 6d.

The arrears are made up as follows:—

		£	s.	d.
8 instalments which fell due in 1877, amounting to	. .	4	12	0
17 " 1878, "	. .	21	0	5
14 " 1879, "	. .	25	9	0
16 " 1880, "	. .	29	9	4
24 " 1881, "	. .	41	8	4
13 " 1882, "	. .	21	11	6
15 " 1883, "	. .	22	3	5
25 " 1884, "	. .	31	19	1
46 " 1885, "	. .	60	5	3
	Total, 168 instalments due, amounting to	£283	19	10

Some of the money now due, I fear, will never be recovered. My reasons for saying this were given in former reports. Since the Board appointed a very active delegate to collect instalments and to represent them in a part of this county, the arrears have diminished and I think will not be permitted to increase, and that some of the old ones may be recovered. It is a misfortune that such a person was not appointed long ago.

The total amount issued in this county for the eleven years up to 31st December, 1885, was £9,267 8s. The amount repaid to 31st December, 1885, according to Board of Works return, was £6,243 17s. 9d. The outstanding promissory notes not arrived at maturity according to the same return amounted to £2,978 4s. 11d.

County Galway.

There were 470 applications received from 672 persons for loans amounting to £7,893 10s. Out of these, 303 loans to 412 people were recommended to the amount of £4,191. The sum of £2,772 has been issued up to the date of this report, 23 of the loans amounting to £419 were cancelled. The loans ranged from £5 to £100.

By the return from the Board of Works the following instalments appear to be in arrears:—

		£	s.	d.
In the case of 3 loans made in 1875, amounting to	. . . .	5	19	1
" 6 " 1876, "	. . . .	20	5	0
" 7 " 1877, "	. . . .	20	5	4
" 16 " 1878, "	. . . .	53	14	0
" 17 " 1879, "	. . . .	138	17	10
" 23 " 1880, "	. . . .	150	5	10
" 15 " 1881, "	. . . .	93	5	9
" 10 " 1882, "	. . . .	37	3	3
" 8 " 1883, "	. . . .	37	9	8
" 11 " 1884, "	. . . .	25	2	8
" 2 " 1885, "	. . . .	3	15	0
Add balance loan cancelled in 1876 and not since paid,	. . . .	4	17	11
" " " 1880 " "	. . . .	36	13	3
" " " 1881 " "	. . .	6	17	2
	Total arrears, . . .	£661	5	6

out of a sum of £17,429 17s. lent, the interest on which amounted to £1,105 16s. 2d.

The arrears are made up of the following instalments overdue:—

		£	s.	d.
6 instalments which fell due in	1878, amounting to	11	5	3
13 " "	1879, "	29	18	10
30 " "	1880, "	58	17	7
43 " "	1881, "	59	6	9
79 " "	1882, "	118	13	4
74 " "	1883, "	106	13	8
71 " "	1884, "	96	16	5
83 " "	1885, "	161	8	11
Total, 416 instalments, amounting to		£643	10	8

The total amount issued in this county for the eleven years was £17,429 17s. The amount repaid, according to Board of Works return to 31st December, 1885, was £10,474 8s. 8d. The outstanding promissory notes, not arrived at maturity, according to the same return, amounted to £7,400 0s. 5d.

County Limerick.

Two applications were received for £41, both of which were recommended.

The total amount of loans made in this county for the eleven years was £[illegible], out of which there remain unpaid promissory notes, not arrived at maturity, £9 13s. [illegible]d.

There are no arrears.

County Clare.

There were 10 applications from 22 persons for loans amounting to £847, out of which 7 loans to 9 persons, amounting to £114 were recommended. The sum of £109 was issued up to date of this report, and one loan of £12 was cancelled. The loans ranged from £6 to £25.

In a great many instances the fishermen in this county have been enabled, by these loans, to make considerable profits, and, without them, they should have abandoned fishing.

By the return received from the Board of Works the following instalments appear to be in arrears:

		£	s.	d.
In the case of 1 loan made in	1875, amounting to	2	5	0
" 5 "	1876, "	15	4	11
" 6 "	1877, "	15	6	7
" 3 "	1878, "	3	10	0
" 8 "	1880, "	1	12	8
" 11 "	1881, "	25	5	6
" 10 "	1882, "	18	18	11
" 7 "	1883, "	18	16	7
" 3 "	1884, "	3	1	8
" 1 "	1885, "	1	11	11
Add loan recalled in 1877 and not since paid,		14	8	6
Total arrears,		£116	18	6

Out of £4,000 18s. loans issued, the interest on which, up to 31st December, 1885, amounted to £234 17s. 10d.

The arrears are made up of the following:—

		£	s.	d.
4 instalments that fell due in	1878 amounting to	1	15	11
9 " "	1879 "	12	7	0
11 " "	1880 "	15	4	1
3 " "	1881 "	5	18	6
5 " "	1882 "	5	12	6
5 " "	1884 "	3	8	7
34 " "	1885 "	61	11	3
Total, 71 instalments, amounting to		£100	7	0

Very little of the amount stated to be due cannot be recovered if active steps taken to compel defaulters to pay. There is no reason for allowing the arrears in this county to be what they are.

The total amount of loans in this county for the eleven years was £4,000 18s., and the amount repaid, according to Board of Works return up to 31st December, 1885, was £3,394 14s. [illegible]d. The outstanding promissory notes, according to the same return, not arrived at maturity, amounted to £326 3s. 6d.

County Kerry.

From that part of the county of Kerry situated in my district there were eight applications received for £772, out of which loans were recommended and issued amounting to £371 11s. One loan of £300 being for oyster cultivation.

General Remarks.

This Act has now been in operation for eleven years, and the following is a general summary up to 31st December, 1885, in the counties of Leitrim, Sligo, Mayo, Galway, Clare, and Limerick, being my district, compiled from Board of Works Return to Parliament, 22nd January, 1886:—

County	Amount of Loans.	[illegible]	[illegible]	[illegible]	[illegible]	[illegible]	[illegible]
	£ s. d.	[illegible]	[illegible]	[illegible]	[illegible]	[illegible]	[illegible]
Leitrim,	[illegible]	[illegible]	[illegible]	[illegible]	[illegible]	—	[illegible]
Sligo,	[illegible]	[illegible]	[illegible]	[illegible]	[illegible]	[illegible]	[illegible]
Mayo,	[illegible]	[illegible]	[illegible]	[illegible]	[illegible]	[illegible]	[illegible]
Galway,	[illegible]	[illegible]	[illegible]	[illegible]	[illegible]	[illegible]	[illegible]
Clare,	[illegible]	[illegible]	[illegible]	[illegible]	[illegible]	[illegible]	[illegible]
Limerick,	[illegible]	[illegible]	[illegible]	[illegible]	[illegible]	[illegible]	[illegible]
Total,	[illegible]	[illegible]	[illegible]	[illegible]	[illegible]	[illegible]	[illegible]

Even assuming the arrears due to be [illegible], and all arrears to be bad debts, the amount of interest on loans exceeds the arrears in these counties by a sum of £1,093 15s. 5d., and in the whole of the eight counties to which this fund is applicable by a sum of £[illegible] 12s. 8d., so that since eleven years since the general fund has considerably increased.

	£	s.	d.
The total loans for the eleven years to 31st December, 1885, amounted to	53,943	7	9
The promissory notes given for these loans amounted to	59,721	9	11
The excess between loans and notes, which represents interest, is	5,778	2	2
The repayments made have been	51,453	3	7
The outstanding notes not yet arrived at maturity amount to	[illegible]	17	10
The amount overdue	1,860	9	6
The amount of interest exceeds the amount overdue by	[illegible]	[illegible]	8

In former reports I referred to the general question of arrears of instalments.

I have yet to add that there are two separate funds, "The Irish Reproductive Loan Fund" and "The Sea Coast Fund," requiring distinct and separate forms, books, and accounts, entailing on this department, already overworked, extra labour and expense, which by their amalgamation could be avoided. With this amalgamation a large sum of money available for counties, from which few applications emanate, might be set free, and made useful for supplying the wants of other counties not sufficiently provided for. There is no valid reason why both funds should not now be made one common fund applicable to the whole coast.

I cannot conclude my report without expressing my best thanks to the officers and men of the Coastguard Service in particular, from whom I have invariably received the most cordial and active co-operation in administering this fund, and without whose valuable assistance difficulties of no ordinary character would have arisen.

THOMAS F. BRADY.

REPRODUCTIVE LOAN FUND.

Major Hayes' Report for the County of Cork, and that part of the County of Kerry situated between Brandon Head and Dursey Island.

County Cork.

Forty-three applications were received during 1885 for loans from 67 persons for a total amount of £1,368 10s. Twenty-three of these were recommended for 41 persons for loans amounting to £616 10s. The remainder for various reasons were necessarily declined.

Since the Fund was made available for fishery loans, in 1874, loans to fishermen in the County of Cork have been made to the amount of £14,884 up to 31st December, 1885.

The repayments of instalments due up to the present have been very satisfactory, total in arrears from the county being only £195 0s. 6d., a considerable portion of which may be recovered.

County Kerry.

Seventy-six applications were received from 102 persons for a total sum of £1,098 5s. Fifty of these were recommended for sixty-six persons for a gross sum of £516 5s. The total amount advanced to fishermen since 1874 is £16,314 4s. 9d., and the instalments in arrear up to 31st December, amounted to £692 11s. 10d., the greater portion of which may be recovered.

SEA AND COAST FISHERIES FUND.

County Waterford.

Eleven applications were received for loans amounting in the aggregate to £994 from 19 applicants. Seven loans were recommended for 10 applicants for a total sum of £408 0s. 0d. The remaining applications could not be recommended.

County Wexford.

Eight applications from thirteen persons were received for advances amounting to £145 1s. 3d.; seven of these from 12 persons were recommended for a total sum of £137. In the remaining case the application could not be recommended.

County Wicklow.

Two applications were received from two applicants, one for a loan of £250, the other for £15. The former had to be refused—and the £15 was recommended.

County Clare.

Fourteen applications were sent in from 31 persons for £2,081. Ten of these from 17 persons were recommended for £1,134, the remainder were refused.

The amount of money available from the Reproductive Loan Fund being insufficient to meet the demands upon it, was supplemented by £1,134 from the Sea Fishery Fund.

There being reason to believe that the money has, in the great majority of cases, been properly applied—indeed I may say that I am nearly certain it has been—as in most cases, the loans recommended have been paid to the parties supplying the boats or gear direct on satisfactory proof being previously given of the different articles having been supplied—and not to the borrowers themselves.

JOS. HAYES.

MR. HORNSBY'S REPORT.

Sea and Coast Fisheries Fund.

County Antrim.

During the year 1885, there were 6 applications for loans received from 10 persons, amounting to £292. Four of these to 5 persons were recommended for a total sum of £147.

County Donegal.

In this county there were 131 applications from 172 persons, amounting to £3,202 7s., out of which 75 loans to 90 persons to the amount of £995 16s. were recommended.

County Down.

Four applications received, amounting to £160, of which 3 to the amount of £132 were recommended.

County Dublin.

Four applications amounting to £1,670 were received during the year, all of which were recommended for the full amount applied for.

County Louth.

Four applications received for the sum of £46, three of which, amounting to £36, were recommended.

From the other counties in my Division, viz., Meath and Londonderry, no applications were received during the year.

The loans granted in the above cases ranged from £5 to £300, and were in most instances paid to the persons supplying the boats and gear, and in this way the due application of the money for fishing purposes was secured.

ALAN HORNSBY.

SALMON FISHERIES.

MR. HORNSBY'S REPORT.

Division extends from Wicklow Head to Mullaghmore, Co. Sligo, embracing in whole or part the counties of Wicklow, Dublin, Kildare, King's County, Meath, Westmeath, Louth, Cavan, Longford, Monaghan, Down, Armagh, Antrim, Londonderry, Fermanagh, Tyrone, Donegal, Leitrim, and Sligo, and including the eight Districts of Dublin, Drogheda, Dundalk, Ballycastle, Coleraine, Londonderry, Letterkenny, and Ballyshannon.

All bye-laws and orders relating to close season, definitions, &c., will be found in the appendices, pages 67 to 76.

No. 1, or Dublin District.

Extends from Wicklow Head to Skerries, county Dublin.

The number of engines in this district remains about the same. An increase has taken place in licenses for salmon rods, there being 125 taken out in 1885, as against 115 in 1884. The number of draft net licenses has decreased by three; pole nets, one.

The receipts were less by a few pounds. But the Board have to their credit in bank a sum of £385 7s. 1d. exclusive of their income for 1885.

The average weight of salmon was 10 lbs.; grilse, 7 lbs.

The take of salmon was less productive than in 1884, although large numbers of fish were observed in the Liffey in July.

The quantity of breeding fish was greater than the preceding year, and no signs of disease were observed. The highest price realized was 2s., and the lowest 10d.

Migrations of smolts occurred in May and June, but no smolts were observed in the rivers as late as September and October.

Grilse were first taken in June, the greatest capture being about middle of July, and in June and July salmon were captured with the grilse, and were somewhat lighter and of a reddish colour.

The greatest quantities of salmon were captured in April and May, and the capture of grilse was about seven for one salmon [illegible].

The chief runs of salmon occurred in August, and of grilse in July.

Spent fish were not observed in February and March, and no foul fish in October.

There were no cases of poisoning rivers.

£13 was expended in protection during close time 1884-5. £47 in open season 1885. £40 of this was in the upper or freshwater division, and £7 in the tidal or lower division.

£333 7s. 1d. was handed over to the new Board, October, 1885.

Six water bailiffs employed by the Conservators throughout the whole year, and three for one to four months—six by private individuals.

Eight persons were prosecuted for breaches of the Fishery Laws, and convictions obtained in all cases but one (a case in the Bray river). Offences against the Fishery Laws have, however, diminished, owing to the vigilance of the Royal Irish Constabulary and the water bailiffs employed by the Board.

No. 13, or Ballyshannon District.

Extends from Rossan Point, county Donegal, to Mullaghmore, county Sligo.

There has been a slight increase in the numbers of licenses taken out in this district, which are now 140 rod licenses, ten cross lines, thirty-three draft net licenses, four pole nets, one stake weir, thirty-two gaps, eleven baskets. The revenue, including £21 1s. 6d. for sale of forfeited engines and interest; £243 14s. 9d. subscriptions, and balances in bank and hands of clerk amounted to £1,073 8s. 7d.

Rod fishings remain the same in value.

Grilse were first taken in the middle of May, but in June the largest capture took place. During the first run of grilse, salmon ran also, and as a rule, were larger than those captured at other periods.

The greatest quantities of salmon were taken in May, and the proportion of the grilse captured to the salmon was about ten to one.

Male and female salmon captured in about equal numbers, and the chief runs occurred in May; those of grilse in June.

No signs of disease were observable.

Angling for trout is prohibited during descent of fry to the sea.

The amount expended in protection was £345 1s.; money handed over to new Board, £[illegible] 13s. 9d.; £204 11s. 2d. in bank, and £34 3s. 7d. in hands of clerk.

Not nearly so many spent fish were destroyed in February and March as formerly, or so many [illegible] fish in October.

There were no cases of poisoning rivers.

The actual revenue, £613, was about the same as the previous year.

The average weight of salmon was about 11 lbs.

The highest price was 1s. 10d. per lb.; lowest, 6d.

The season was much more productive and the quantity of breeding fish was much greater than in the preceding year.

Offences against Fishery Laws diminished. 231 bailiffs were employed by the Board.

There were twenty-three prosecutions by the water bailiffs, and six by members of the Royal Irish Constabulary.

No. 14, or Letterkenny District.

Extends from Malin Head to Rossan Point, county Donegal.

The number of engines for which licenses were issued in this district was slightly greater than in 1884, there being ninety-six rod licenses, eleven draft nets, eighteen drift nets, three bag nets, seven [illegible] of baskets, three boxes, twenty-six [illegible]. Total receipts, £[illegible] 10s., as against £213 in 1884.

The average weight of salmon about 10 lbs., and of grilse about 6 lbs.—the weight remaining much the same as in 1884.

The highest price given was 2s., and the lowest, 6d. per lb.

The take of salmon and grilse was greater than in 1884. Fish especially observed to be more numerous from end of May to end of June.

Rod fishings have increased about thirty-five per cent., of which the rentals amounted to about £90.

There was a good supply of breeding fish in 1885, being about the same as in 1884, and no sign of salmon disease observed.

Not many spent fish destroyed in February or March, but a few in October.

Offences against the Fishery Laws have diminished, there being thirty prosecutions instituted by the Board of Conservators, fourteen of which were proved by members of the Royal Irish Constabulary, and three prosecutions were conducted by that force.

Four water bailiffs were employed by Conservators during the entire year.

£824 was handed over to the new Board by the outgoing Board in 1885.

One hundred and six bailiffs are employed by individuals during the close time, and seventy-eight during the open season, at from £1 10s. to £14 per man per annum.

Bailiffs are employed by the Marquis Conyngham, Earl of Leitrim, Lord [illegible], Sir A. Stewart, Bart., Colonel Tredennick, Messrs. W. Olphert, Richardson, Stewart, [illegible], [illegible], and Captain [illegible].

In consequence of applications received, we held two inquiries. 1.—To inquire into the subject of changing the season for salmon and trout in the Owena and [illegible] Rivers. 2.—To consider the desirability of changing the close time for salmon and trout in Trawbreaga Bay. After hearing the evidence tendered to us, we decided upon changing those seasons as requested, making the close season for the Owena and [illegible] Rivers to commence on 1st September and end on 31st May, and that for Trawbreaga Bay to commence on 1st October and end on 30th June.

The Conservators suggested that the law be amended so as to authorize the seizure of and forfeiture of unlicensed nets when found in possession of persons or concealed in houses near rivers or lakes.

No. 15, Londonderry District.

Extends from Downhill boundary, county Derry, to Malin Head, county Donegal.

The number of licensed engines in this district varies but little from that in 1884. A slight increase in salmon rods, being 101, as against 93 in 1884; a decrease in cross lines, being 6, as against 11; a decrease of 2 drift nets, being 55, as against 57; also, a decrease of 1 stake net and 1 pole net.

Amount received for licence duty, £534; for fines, £18 2s. 4d.; poor rate valuation,

£95; subscriptions from lessees of the Hon. the Irish Society's Fishery in Lough and River Foyle, £620. Total revenue, £1,438 18s. 8d.

The average weight of salmon was 11 lbs.; of peals, 6 lbs., and the highest price given was 1s. 6d.; the lowest, 5d.

The take of salmon and grilse was more productive in 1885 than in 1884, although the quantity of breeding fish was about the same.

Grilse were first taken end of May; the largest quantity was observed in July, and salmon were taken with the grilse in July and August. These salmon were rather lighter than in June, the largest quantities of salmon taken in July and August, and no signs of disease observed in the district.

Angling for trout was not prohibited by any proprietor during the descent of fry; considerable numbers were caught.

Large numbers of spent fish were formerly destroyed in February and March, but not since the change of close time. A number of full fish are taken by anglers in October.

No cases of poisoning rivers have been detected in the district.

Offences against the fishery laws have increased, there being 41 prosecutions instituted by the Royal Irish Constabulary, and 10 by the Board of Conservators.

During close season, 1884-5, £930 was expended in protection; during open season 1885, £210 was expended, of this £1,090 was expended in the upper or freshwater division; £140 in the tidal and lower divisions.

The amount handed over to the new Board in 1885 was £111 10s. 2d. The whole of this amount was in bank.

About forty bailiffs were employed in the district by private individuals (lessees of the Hon. the Irish Society) and 240 by the Board of Conservators, majority of whom were for six months and some for whole year.

Wages varied from £3 to £21, according to the time employed.

No proprietors in upper waters contribute funds towards protection.

No. 15b, or Coleraine District.

Extends from Portrush, county Antrim, to Downhill boundary, county of Londonderry.

There was an increase in the number of licences taken out in this district, there being 172 single rod licences, as against 100 in 1884; 162 draft nets, as against 120 in 1884; 138 trammel nets, as against 103 in 1884; 86 cogbills, as against 55 in 1884; 9 drift nets, as against 3 in 1884. There was a decrease of 1 box, there being 5 in 1884.

The revenue of the district consisted of £1,091 licence duty; £20 14s. 6d. proportion of fines; £3 16s. 6d. sale of forfeited engines; £276 rate on poor law valuation; making a total of £1,391 5s. 10d.

The largest salmon taken was 38 lbs. The highest price realised was 2s. per lb.; the lowest, 6d.; and the capture was fully one half more than in 1884. The first salmon was taken on 20th March.

The quantity of breeding fish was believed to be much the same as in 1884.

Grilse were first taken during the first week of May. The greatest quantity being observed from about the 23rd of June to the 20th July, and salmon were taken with the grilse in the latter end of June and in July, and these salmon were on an average larger than those at other periods.

The greatest quantities of salmon were taken in May, and the chief runs occurred in May, June, and July.

No signs of disease have been observed.

Angling for trout is not prohibited during descent of salmon fry to the sea, but scarcely any destruction of fry takes place.

There were not many spent fish caught in months of July and February, but a good many full fish were taken in October.

A good deal of injury is done by flax water being allowed to flow into the rivers, and the magistrates are most unwilling to convict in cases where the Conservators prosecute, the result being the board spend large sums in prosecutions, and very often with little or no result.

There was also a case of poisoning by deleterious matter being permitted to flow from a soap factory.

Offences against the fishery laws have remained much the same, there having been about 52 prosecutions instituted by the Conservators and 4 by the Royal Irish Constabulary.

The number of water-bailiffs employed by the Board is 38 (and 7 inspectors); one at £5 and one at £6, and the remaining 36 at from £8 to £20 per annum.

The amount expended by the Board in protection during half-year from 1st October, 1884, to 1st April, 1885, was £481 8s., and during that from 1st April, 1885, to 1st October, 1885, £[illegible] 0s. 9d. The whole of these amounts with the exception of about £60 in each half-year were expended on the upper or fresh-water division of the district.

After paying all salaries and accounts for the two half years there was a balance in bank in October, 1885, of £[illegible] [illegible] 11d.; in hands of clerk, £11 6s. 2d. Total, £297 9s. 1d.

About 12 private water bailiffs are employed in the district, 6 of whom are employed by the Foyle and Bann Fishery Company at from £5 to £12 for the close time (three months).

Others are employed by Sir J. [illegible], Bart., Fishing Club at Blackwater, and Bann Fishery Club.

No. 16. Ballycastle District.

Extends from Donaghadee, county Down, to Portrush, county Antrim.

There was a slight falling off in the number of licensed engines fished in this district in 1885. Being 19 rods, 19 trammel nets, 14 bag nets, 1 coghill, as against 23 rods, 12 trammel nets, 14 bag nets, and 1 coghill in 1884.

The revenue of the district was £195 10s. licence duty, 12s. 1d. fines, and £29 subscriptions. Total, £225 3s. 1d.

The highest price given for salmon was 2s. 4d., and the lowest, 6½d. There was an average supply of breeding fish, and the take was about the same as in 1884.

Grilse were taken in April and May in largest quantities.

No appreciable signs of disease have been observed.

More or less destruction of salmon fry takes place by trout fishing during the descent to the sea, but spent fish were not destroyed.

No cases of poisoning have been reported. Some cases of flax water pollution have been noticed.

No prosecutions were instituted by the Conservators, and none by the Royal Irish Constabulary.

£331 7s. was expended by the Conservators on protection, nearly all being upon the upper waters.

Seven permanent bailiffs were paid by the Board, and 15 temporary, but no private water bailiffs were employed, and no upper water proprietors contribute towards protection.

No. 17. Dundalk District.

Extends from Clogher Head, county Louth, to Donaghadee, county Down.

There was a decrease in the number of licences issued for single rods, 94 being taken out, and 109 in 1884; a decrease in the number of draft net licences by 3; an increase in the number of licences for gaps, eyes, or baskets, being 35, as against 13 in 1884; bag net and stake weir licences remain unaltered.

The revenue of the district was—licence duty, £269; fines received, £23 0s. 9d.; sale of forfeited engines, 4s.; rates on poor law valuation, £18 10s. Total, £804 14s. 9d.

The average weight of salmon was 14 lbs., and of peale, 5 lbs.; and the highest price realized was 2s per lb., the lowest, 6d.

The take of salmon throughout the district was somewhat less than in 1884; this may be attributed to the dry season and few spates, but the quantity of breeding fish observed was greater.

Rod fishings have not increased in value; one is let at £4 4s. per annum, and another at £17 per annum.

Only one migration of smolts to the sea was observed during the season.

Grilse were first taken in June and the largest capture took place in August, and salmon were taken with the grilse in July. These salmon were on an average lighter than at other periods; but it is difficult to say when the greatest quantities were captured, probably April or May.

No signs of disease have been observed.

Little or no destruction of fry takes place during its descent to the sea by trout fishers.

Not many spent fish destroyed in the months of February or March.

There have been a few cases of flax water being permitted to flow into rivers, and in the Rostrevor river dye stuff from mills was allowed to escape.

Offences against the fishery laws have diminished.

Thirty-one prosecutions were instituted by the Conservators, ten by the members of the Royal Irish Constabulary, and twelve by private individuals.

The highest number of water bailiffs employed during the year is 14; the lowest, 8; they are paid £1 4s. a month when employed.

During the close season, 1884–5, £80 was expended in protection, and during the open season, 1885, £167 13s.

Of this £96 5s. was in 1884 spent on upper water, and £93 10s. in 1885. In tidal waters £13 was expended.

Eight water bailiffs were employed by private individuals, and water keepers were also employed by Lord Rathdonnell, John Woolsey, William D. Filgate, Esqrs., the Earl of Kilmorey, Arthur Macan, and H. O'Reilly Dease, Esqrs.

No. 17. Drogheda District.

Extends from Skerries, county Dublin, to Clogher Head, county Louth.

There was an increase in the number of engines licensed in this district in 1885, there being 144 salmon rods, 7 cross lines, 3 snap-nets, 134 draft nets, 6 boxes or cribs, and 31 gaps or eyes.

The revenue was composed of—License duty, £682 10s.; amount of fines, £5 13s. 8d.; amount realised by sale of forfeited engines, 13s. Total, £692 1s. 8d.

The average weight of salmon was 14 lbs., and of peals, 5 lbs., and the highest price given for salmon was 2s. 6d. and the lowest, 8d. per lb.

The take of salmon and grilse was, on the whole, better than in 1884, and the quantity of breeding fish observed in the rivers within the district was about the same.

Three migrations of smolts to the sea were observed—one in May, one in June, and one in July.

Smolts were not observed migrating so late as September and October.

Grilse were first captured early in June, but the greatest quantity was taken in July.

Some large salmon were taken with grilse in beginning of August, but they are not so heavy as the spring fish.

The greatest quantity of salmon were taken in April, and it is believed there were more salmon than grilse captured.

The number of female fish captured exceed the number of male, and little or no disease has been observed in the district.

Trout fishing is not prevented during the descent of the fry to the sea, and no doubt some are taken, but no spent fish were destroyed by anglers in February or March, and no full fish to any extent were taken in October.

There have been no cases of poisoning any of the rivers in this district.

Offences against the Fishery Laws have diminished, there being been only four or five cases of breaches of the law throughout the whole district in the past year.

No funds were contributed through the Board of Conservators for the purposes of protection, and the Clerk reports his Board have no knowledge of the number of water bailiffs employed by private individuals.

Concluding Observations.

The capture in the tidal waters of the Northern portion of my Division was larger than it has been for a number of years.

ALAN HORNSBY.

MR. BRADY'S REPORT

On Division of Ireland extending from Dunmore Head, in the county of Kerry, to Mullaghmore, in the county of Sligo, embracing in the whole or part the counties of Kerry, Clare, Limerick, Tipperary, King's, Queen's, Galway, Longford, Westmeath, Roscommon, Leitrim, Mayo, Cavan, and Sligo.

No. 8, or Limerick District.

Extends from Dunmore Head, in the County of Kerry, to Hag's Head, in the county of Clare, and includes all that part of the country the waters of which flow into the sea coast between those points.

Close Seasons.

The close seasons in this district are—For tidal and fresh waters:

* Between 31st July and 12th February, save river Cashen, and Tralee [illegible] and [illegible] River, and [illegible] Kerry [illegible] Dunmore Head and [illegible] Head and Hag's Head, and all [illegible] flowing into the sea between those points.

"For Cashen, down to its mouth and [illegible], between 31st August and 1st June. For Maigue River, between 15th July and 1st February; between Dunmore Head and Kerry Head, and all rivers flowing into the sea between those points, between 15th September and 1st April; between Loop Head and Hag's Head, and all rivers running into the sea between those points, between 15th September and 1st May."

For angling with single rods and lines:—

"Between 31st September and 1st February, over Shannon, [illegible], Deel, Cashen, and [illegible] [illegible], and [illegible] [illegible]; and over all rivers running into the sea between Loop Head and Hag's Head, and between Dunmore Head and Kerry Head. For Feale, Geale, Cashen and [illegible], between 31st October and 17th March. For Shannon and [illegible] [illegible] and its [illegible], between 31st October and 1st February; between Loop Head and Hag's Head, between 30th September and 1st March, and between Dunmore Head and Kerry Head, between 30th September and 1st April."

By-laws.

The by-laws in force in the district are as follows:—

In River Shannon:

"Prohibiting net fishing in that part of the River Shannon between Wellesley-bridge and the Railway bridge, between 1st June and 12th February.

"Prohibiting between the 1st day of August, or such other day as may be the first day of the close season, and the 1st day of November in each year, the use of draft nets, or any other net or nets used as a draft net, having a foot-rope and leads or weights affixed thereto, within the following limits, viz.:—In that part of the River Shannon which lies between the Fishing weir known as the Lax Weir, and a line drawn due north and south across the said River Shannon at the western extremity of Graigue Island.

"Prohibiting draft nets for the capture of fish of any kind, of a mesh less than one and three-quarter inches from knot to knot, to be measured along the side of the square, or seven inches to be measured all round each such mesh, such measurements being taken in the clear when the net is wet, in the tidal parts of the River Shannon, or in the tidal parts of any of the rivers flowing into the said River Shannon.

"Prohibiting the fishing for salmon or trout by any means whatsoever, within a space of twenty yards from the weir wall of Thomondgate(?), on the River Shannon.

"Prohibiting having nets for capture of salmon or trout on board any cot or curragh between mouth of Shannon and Wellesley-bridge, in the city of Limerick, or in tidal parts of any rivers flowing into the said River Shannon between said points, between the hours of nine o'clock on Saturday morning and three o'clock on Monday morning; or between Wellesley-bridge and the Navigation Weir at Killaloe, in the county of Clare, between eight o'clock on Saturday morning and four o'clock on Monday morning.

"Prohibiting the shooting of fish in that part of River Shannon between Portumna-bridge, and Shannon-bridge."

In River Shannon and Clonderlaw Bay:—

"Regulating the use of drift nets as follows:—

"First.—That no drift nets of greater length than 100 yards shall be used for the capture of salmon or trout in any part of the River Shannon between Limerick and a line drawn across the river below Askeaton, from Aughinish Point, in the county of Limerick, to Kildysart in the county of Clare.

"Second.—That no drift nets of greater length than 200 yards shall be used for the capture of salmon or trout in any other tidal waters of the River Shannon, or in Clonderlaw Bay.

"Third.—That no two or more drift nets shall be attached together in any way or be allowed to drift within 150 yards of each other in the River Shannon, or in Clonderlaw Bay.

"Fourth.—That no drift nets below, or eastward of a line drawn across the River Shannon, from Aughinish Point, in the county of Limerick, to Kildysart, in the county of Clare, shall be used within the line of low-water mark of ordinary spring tides.

"Fifth.—That no drift nets shall be used in Clonderlaw Bay above a line drawn from Knock to Lachmoheloo(?) in the county of Clare.

"That no drift nets shall be used in the Rivers Maigue or Askeaton."

In Lough Ree:—

"Permitting the use of nets, having a mesh of five inches in the round, measured when the net is wet."

In River Fergus:—

"Prohibiting the fishing for salmon or trout by any means whatsoever, within a space of twenty yards from the weir wall at Ennis.

"Prohibiting the use of drift nets in the tidal parts of River."

In River Maigue:—

"Prohibiting the use of draft nets between a line drawn across said river at the southern boundary of the townland of Ballyressy(?) to the opposite shore on the townland of Clonsuma(?) and the old bridge of Adare.

"Prohibiting use of all nets, except landing nets as auxiliary to rod and line, above Railway bridge below Adare.

"Prohibiting the use of drift nets.

"Prohibiting the shooting of fish."

In Lough Derg:—

"Permitting the use of nets not exceeding twelve yards in length, with meshes of one inch from knot to knot for the capture of fish other than salmon and trout.

"Prohibiting the use of nets (except landing nets as auxiliary to angling with rod and line) for the capture of fish other than eels, between eight o'clock in the evening and six o'clock in the morning."

In River Deel or Askeaton:—

"Prohibiting the use of [illegible] nets.

"Prohibiting the use of all nets (except landing nets as auxiliary to angling with rod and line) for the capture of salmon or trout in that part of the river which lies between [illegible] and the mouth of River [illegible]."

In River Mulkear:—

"Prohibiting fishing for salmon or trout within fifty yards below Mill Weir at Ballyclough."

The principal rivers in the Limerick District, and their seasons for Netting and Angling for Salmon and Trout, are as follows:—

River.	Net Fishing.	Freshwater [illegible]	Angling, Single Rod and Line.
Cashen,	1st June to 31st August, inclusive,	Same as Tidal,	15th March to 31st Oct., inclusive.
Feale,	1st April to 15th Sept., do.,	do.,	1st April to 30th Sept., do.
Deel or Askeaton,	Not allowed,	do.,	1st February to 30th Sept., do.
Doonbeg,	1st May to 15th Sept., inclusive,	do.,	1st March to 30th Sept., do.
Ennistymon or Inagh,	Do. do.,	do.,	Do. do.
Fergus,	12th Feb. to 31st July, do.,	do.,	1st February to 30th Sept., do.
Maigue,	1st Feb. to 15th July, do.,	do.,	1st February to 30th Sept., do.
Shannon,	12th Feb. to 31st July, do.,	do.,	1st February to 31st Oct., do.
Mulkear,	Do. do.,	do.,	Do. do.

Report.

The state of the fisheries in the district is reported as prosperous. The take of fish was more productive than in the preceding year. The quantity of breeding fish observed was greater. Numbers of very large fish in 1885—the average weight of the salmon was 16 lbs.; that of grilse 6 lbs. Angling is carried on during the descent of salmon fry; but it is not considered that much destruction of fry takes place, nor are many spent fish destroyed; but it is thought that a large number of full or breeding fish are taken during the month of October.

There has been reported only one case of poisoning, which occurred on the river Feale by lime. According to the returns, there were 71 water-bailiffs employed during the open season, between 1st February, 1885, and October, 1885; and 107 during the close season, between October, 1885, and February, 1886. The amount paid for protection in the breeding season, October, 1884, to February, 1885, was £748, and the amount paid during the open season of 1885, i.e., from February to October, £720. Of the total amount, the sum expended on the upper waters by the Conservators was £1,131, and on the tidal waters £279.

No water-bailiffs are known to be employed by private individuals, and only one gentleman subscribed a sum of £5 towards protection; while out of this extensive district there was only a sum of £17 5s. paid as rates on the Poor Law Valuation. There were only 18 prosecutions by the Board, viz.:—

For using strokehaul,	2
" " gaffs and lights,	6
" " nets in fresh water,	1
" angling without licences,	3
" taking unseasonable fish,	2
" obstructing gap in mill weir,	1
" breach of weekly close season,	2
" " of [illegible],	2

So that there were actually very few offences against the important interests or prosperity of the fisheries apparently committed, or, if committed, not brought to justice. The amount of fines imposed for these offences came to £10 15s.—one case was dismissed, and another reversed on appeal.

There were 15 offences prosecuted by the Constabulary, and fines imposed in 14 cases, one of them having been dismissed, amounted to £21 4s. They were for:—

Breaches of the close season,	12
" of the weekly close season,	1
Killing unseasonable fish,	1
" fish illegally,	1

There were 2 cases, breaches of the weekly close season, prosecuted by the Coast Guard. In the whole year the number of prosecutions reported was 35, of which the Conservators had 18—the Constabulary 15, and the Coast Guard 2.

If this be a correct state of the district, it speaks well of the observance of the law in general. If it be not, then little value is given for such a large number of men employed, and money expended.

	£
The amount paid to water-bailiffs during the year was,	4,471
" " for expenses of prosecutions,	[illegible]
" " for travelling and miscellaneous expenses,	318
" " for salaries,	600
" " for commission on sale of licenses,	138
" " for postage and printing, &c.,	81
" " as prosecutors' moieties of penalties,	50

The revenue of the year was derived from licenses sold, viz.: 279 salmon rods, 57 cross lines, 36 snap nets, 51 draft nets, 128 drift nets, 28 pole nets, 43 stake nets, 18 boxes or cribs, and 275 gaps or eyes for taking eels, and these amounted to £2,667.

	£
To which is to be added for fines,	18
" " " rates on Poor Law Valuation,	57
" " " balance on bank account,	10
" " " subscriptions,	8
" " " donations,	4
Total,	£2,[illegible]

This year a number of additional queries were put to the Conservators, with the view of obtaining information on matters connected with the migration of salmon and grilse, the proportions of male and female fish taken, the different runs of salmon and grilse from the sea during the year, the proportion the capture of grilse bears to the capture of salmon, and other subjects which it was thought the bailiffs or inspectors might have been able to throw some light on; but the answers have been, "cannot say," "not known," "believe not," "not to my knowledge," so that no information could be elicited.

No. 6. Galway District.

Extends from Hag's Head in the county Clare to Slyne Head in the county Galway, and includes all that part of the county, the waters of which flow into the coast between these two points.

The close seasons in force in the district are as follows:—

For tidal and upper waters:—

"Between 15th August and 1st February, save in Corrib or Galway river and lakes and tributaries between 31st August and 15th February."

For angling with single rods and lines:—

"Between 15th October and 1st February, save in Cashla, Doonkelly, Spiddal, Ballinahinch, Crumlin, Screeb and Inver Rivers and their lakes and tributaries, which is between 31st October and 1st February."

Bye-laws.

The bye-laws in force are:—

In Galway River, and Loughs Corrib and Mask, and Tributaries:—

"Prohibiting the use of the instrument commonly called strokehaul, or snatch, or any other such instrument.

"Prohibiting the use of nets of any kind whatsoever in any part of the rivers known as the Clare and Claregalway or Turloughmore rivers, in the county of Galway, above the junction of said rivers with Lough Corrib.

"Prohibiting the snatching or attempting to snatch salmon in any tidal or fresh waters in the district with any kind of fish hook covered in part or in whole with any matter or thing, or uncovered."

The principal Rivers in the Galway District, and their seasons for Netting and Angling for Salmon and Trout are as follows:—

Rivers	Tidal Netting	Freshwater Netting, &c.	Angling with Single Rod and Line.
Ballinahinch, .	1st Feb. to 15th August, inclusive,	Same as Tidal, .	1st Feb. to 31st October, inclusive.
Cashla, . .	Do do., .	do., .	Do. do.
Crumlin, . .	Do do., .	do., .	Do. do.
Doonkelly, .	Do. do., .	do., .	Do. do.
Galway, . .	15th Feb. to 31st August, do., .	do., .	1st Feb. to 15th October, do.
Inver, . . .	1st Feb to 15th August, do., .	do., .	1st Feb. to 31st October, do.
Kilcolgan, . .	Do. do., .	do., .	1st Feb. to 15th October, do.
Spiddle, . .	Do. do., .	do., .	1st Feb. to 31st October, do.
Screeb, . .	Do. do., .	do., .	Do. do.

In this district the capture of fish during the past year is reported as less. No reason can be assigned. It is suggested that drought may have been the cause. Angling for trout is prohibited, as far as practicable, during the descent of the fry. Few, if any, spent fish are destroyed, but it is stated that considerable numbers of breeding salmon are taken by anglers in October, too full to be fit for the table, and is against increased production.

Offences against the fishery laws have diminished. The quantity of breeding fish during the past season much the same as former one. The average weight of salmon was 12 lbs., that of grilse 6½ lbs.

No sign of disease has appeared.

There are about thirty-five bailiffs employed by the Conservators; one half of these all the year round, the other half from two to three months. Rates of pay from £8 to £10 a year. The amount expended in protection during the breeding or close season was £187, and during the open season £67.

In addition to the bailiffs employed by the Conservators, there are about 230 employed by private individuals, some of these, about two-thirds, from £2 to £20 a year.

A correct return of the number of prosecutions for offences has not been furnished, but according to the accounts a sum of £13 was received on account of fines.

The Licences sold were 132 rods, 14 cross lines, 43 draft nets, 3 trammel nets, 5 boxes or cribs, and 22 gaps or eyes for taking eels, making the revenue £238.

	£
To which is to be added, for Fines,	13
„ „ „ „ Rates on Poor Law Valuation,	56
Total,	251

a sum far short of providing for anything like necessary protection

The expenditure incurred was as follows:—

	£
For Water Bailiffs,	65
„ Travelling, and Miscellaneous Expenses,	50
„ Salaries,	79
„ Postage and Printing,	7
Total,	201

A number of additional queries were put to the Conservators this year, in order to elicit, if possible, some information on matters connected with the salmon fisheries, and the replies given have not been such as might be expected from this district. They are as follows:—It has not been observed that more than one migration of smolts take place, nor a later migration than usual, nor any smolts in rivers during September or October. The first grilse is taken about the 1st May, and the greater quantity is taken in June. Salmon are taken with the grilse in July of lighter weight than in the Spring months, and the greatest quantity of salmon is taken in that month. More female salmon than males are captured. It is difficult to ascertain what proportion the capture of grilse bears to salmon, as they would require to be examined with care by an experienced person. Two runs of salmon, and one of grilse, have been observed—the former in February, March, April and July, and the latter from middle of May to middle of July.

Returns of prosecutions by the Constabulary or Coast Guard have not been received.

10⁴, Ballynakill District,

Extends from Slyne Head, co. Galway, to Pidgeon Point, co. Mayo, and includes all that part of the country the waters of which flow into the coast between those two points.

Close Seasons.

The close seasons in force are as follows:—

In tidal and fresh waters:—

"Between 31st August, and 16th February, save in Louisburgh and Carrownisky rivers and estuaries, which is between 15th September and 1st July."

For angling with single rod:—

"Between 31st October and 1st February, save in Carrownisky river which is between 31st October and 1st July, and save in Louisburgh river, which is between 31st October and 1st June."

There are no special by-laws in the district.

The principal rivers in the Ballinakill District, and the seasons for Netting and Angling for Salmon or Trout are as follows :—

Rivers.	Tidal Netting.	Freshwater Netting.	Angling with Single Rod and Line.
Carrowniskey, . .	1st July to 15th Sept., inclusive, .	Same as Tidal, .	1st July to 31st October, inclusive.
Culfin, . .	15th Feb. to 31st Aug., do. .	do., .	1st Feb. to 31st October, do.
Delphi, . .	Do. do., .	do., .	Do. do.
Dawros at Kylemore, . .	Do. do., .	do., .	Do. do.
Erriff, . .	Do. do., .	do., .	Do. do.
Louisburgh, . .	1st July to 15th Sept., do., .	do., .	1st June to 31st October, do.

The general state of the fisheries in this district was better than in 1884—the take of fish was more productive—the rod fishings have also increased in value, as more licences were taken out.

The quantity of breeding fish during the last close season was greater than the preceding one. No sign of disease has appeared. No poisoning, and no spent fish destroyed.

The offences against the fishery laws are, however, reported as increased.

During the year there have been 24 prosecutions by the Conservators. They were as follows :—

For breaches of the close season, ...	15
For using gaffs, or netting and shooting, ...	9

Of these there were 7 cases acquitted, 15 convicted, and 2 left the country.

There are 20 bailiffs employed—3 being in the open and the rest in the close.

The amount paid for—

	£	s.	d.
Water Bailiffs, &c., ...	65	0	0
Travelling and Miscellaneous Expenses . . .	3	0	0
Salaries and Commission on sale of Licences, .	15	0	0
Expenses of prosecutions, Postage, Printing, &c., .	1	0	0
Aid to Prosecutions	3	10	0

The total revenue was from 60 rod licences, 15 draft nets, and 1 pole net, and amounted to £107.

There are several bailiffs employed by private individuals. No rates on the Poor Law Valuation have been received.

No. 10, or Bangor District.

Extends from Pidgeon Point, co. Mayo, to Benwee Head, and includes all that part of the country the waters of which flow into the ocean between those two points.

Close Seasons.

The close seasons in the district are as follows :—

For tidal and fresh waters :—

"Between the 31st August and 16th February, save in Newport and Glenamoy Rivers and Estuaries; for Newport River and Estuary, 31st August and 20th March; for Glenamoy River and Estuary, 15th September and 1st May.

For angling with single rod and line :—

"Between 30th September and 1st May, save Burrishoole between 31st October and 1st February, Owengarve and Glenamoy between 31st October and 1st May, Owenmore and Munhin between 30th September and 1st February, Owenduff or Ballycroy, and Ballyveeny and Owenduff, and all rivers in Achill Island, between 31st October and 1st February."

Bye-laws.

The bye-laws in force in this district are as follows :—

"Prohibiting the removal of gravel or sand from any part of the bed of the Owenmore River, in the county of Mayo, where the spawning of Salmon or Trout may take place."

"Prohibiting the use of Nets with Meshes of less than one and a half inches from knot to knot (to be measured along the side of the square, or [illegible] inches to be measured all round each mesh, such measurement being taken in the clear when the Net is wet), within the mouth of the said Rivers Owenduff or Ballycroy, Owenmore and Munhin, [illegible] the mouth as defined, during the months of June, July, and August, as the same [illegible] for the capture of Salmon or Trout with Nets, in the said Rivers."

The following are the Principal Rivers in the Bangor District, with the seasons for Netting and Angling for Salmon and Trout:—

Rivers.	Close Season.	Freshwater Netting.	Angling with Single Rod and Line.
Achill Island,	12th Feb. to 31st Aug., inclusive,	None in Tidal,	1st Feb. to 31st October, inclusive.
Ballycroy,	Do. do.,	do.,	Do. do.
Burrishoole,	Do. do.,	do.,	Do. do.
Glenamoy,	1st May to 15th Sept., do.,	do.,	1st May to 31st October, do.
Moyrus,	12th Feb. to 31st Aug., do.,	do.,	1st May to 30th Sept., do.
Munhin,	Do. do.,	do.,	1st Feb. to 30th Sept., do.
Newport,	20th March to 31st Aug., do.,	do.,	1st May to 30th Sept., do.
Owenmore,	12th Feb. to 31st Aug., do.,	do.,	1st Feb. to 30th Sept., do.
Owengarve,	Do. do.,	do.,	1st May to 31st October, do.

The general state of the fisheries in this district is reported as satisfactory. The take of fish in 1885 was more productive than in 1884, though in most rivers it was very inferior. The quantity of breeding fish in rivers was greater in the past than the preceding season. Angling is not carried on during the descent of the salmon fry. No sign of disease has appeared. Spent fish are not destroyed, but some full or breeding fish are killed in October when angling is carried on. Offences against the fishing laws have diminished. There were only 2 prosecutions by the Conservators during the year, 1 for illegal fishing and 1 for breach of the weekly close season.

Amount of fines paid, £2. No returns of prosecutions by Constabulary or Coast-Guard have been received.

There were 53 bailiffs employed during the close and 9 during the open season.

Bailiffs are employed in the Upper portion of Owenmore, &c., by a private individual. Except in this case no proprietors in the upper waters contribute towards protection.

The tidal lessees also employ bailiffs, as the funds of the Board are insufficient for the necessary protection.

The amount expended during the year was:—

	£
For Water Bailiffs,	[illegible]
For Salaries,	47
For Printing, Postage, and Stationery,	10
For Prosecutions, exclusive of penalties,	4

The revenue of the district was made up of licences for 25 rods—25 draft nets and 14 bag nets, and amounted to £246, to which is to be added fines, £4; total, £252.

In answer to the special queries the Board reply, that in some cases there was more than one migration of smolts. They took place in April and May, but no smolts have been observed in September or October. The grilse are first taken in May, and the largest quantity in July. In June salmon are taken with the grilse. Those taken in the bag nets are heavier, but no difference in the estuaries. The greatest quantities of salmon are taken in April, May, and June, but in the Owenmore Fishery in February, March, and April. The proportion of grilse taken compared with salmon is 12 to 1 in one estuary, and about 4 to 1 in others. More male fish are taken in the bag nets, but it is not observed in the estuary fisheries. There is no increase in the average size of the salmon or grilse. In the bag nets the average is 12 lbs. and 5½ lbs. In the estuaries the average is 9 lbs. to 12 lbs., and the grilse 5 lbs. to 6 lbs. No sign of disease has appeared.

No. 11, or Ballina District.

Extends from Benwee Head, in the county of Mayo, to Coonamore Point, in the county of Sligo, and includes all that part of the country the waters of which flow into the coast between those two points.

Close Seasons.

For tidal waters the close seasons in force are:—Netting, between 15th August and 15th March, save Palmerston and Easkey Rivers, which is between 31st August and 1st June.

For upper waters:—Netting, between 31st July and 1st February, save Palmerston and Easkey Rivers, which is between 31st August and 1st June. Angling—between 15th September and 1st February, save Easkey River and tributaries, which is between 31st October and 1st February, and save Cloonaghmore or Palmerston River and tributaries; the tidal parts being between 31st October and 1st February, and upper parts being between 31st October and 1st June.

By-laws.

The by-laws in force are as follows:—

"Permitting use of nets with meshes of one and a quarter inches from knot to knot to be measured along the side of the square, or five inches to be measured all round each such mesh, such measurements being taken in the clear, when the net is wet."

"Prohibiting angling for trout during April and May in each year—Loughs Conn and Cullin excepted."

Killala Bay.—"First—Prohibiting to catch or attempt to catch Salmon or Trout by means of Drift Nets inside or to the southward of a line drawn from the Bath Fort at [illegible], in the county of Sligo, to Ross Point, in the county of Mayo.

"Second—No Drift Nets of greater length than 400 yards shall be used for the capture of Salmon or Trout in any part of the said Bay of Killala, outside or to the northward of said line.

"Third—No two or more Drift Nets shall be attached together in any way in the said Bay of Killala, or to the same boat while fishing in said Bay.

"Fourth—Whenever a Drift Net shall be used for the capture of Salmon or Trout in the said Bay of Killala, it shall be attached to a boat which shall remain over said Net while fishing, and the fishermen engaged in fishing with said Drift Net shall remain on board such boat whilst said Drift Net shall be in the water."

The principal rivers in the Ballina district and the seasons for netting and angling for salmon or trout are as follows:—

Rivers	Tidal Netting	Freshwater Netting	Angling with Single Rod and Line
Ballycastle, .	16th Mar. to 12th Aug., inclusive	1 Feb. & 31 July	1st Feb. to 15th Sept. inclusive
Cloonaghmore or Palmerstown.	1st June to 31st Aug. do. .	Same as Tidal, .	In tidal waters, 1st Feb. to 31st Oct., and in up waters, 1st June to 31st Oct. inclusive.
Easky, . .	1st June to 31st Aug. do. .	do.	1st Feb. to 31st Oct. inclusive.
Moy, . .	16th Mar. to 12th Aug. do. .	1 Feb. & 31 July	1st Feb. to 15th Sept. inclusive.

The state of the fisheries in this district reported as good. The take of both salmon and grilse more productive than preceding year. Grilse were later coming into the river than usual. The quantity of breeding fish observed greater than preceding season. No sign of disease observed. Angling is prohibited during the descent of fry. No case of poisoning. Offences against the fishery laws have decreased last year. There are 34 bailiffs employed by the Conservators during the close season at from £2 to £8, and 7 during the open season, at from £3 to £10. The amount expended in protection during the close season was £270, and during the open season £18. In addition to this, the proprietors of the Moy Tidal Fisheries employed about 200 bailiffs. One proprietor (Sir Charles Knox Gore) only in this extensive district contributes £5 towards protection.

There were 55 prosecutions by the Conservators during the year. These prosecutions are conducted, according to a rule of the Conservators, by the manager of the tidal fisheries of the Moy, and it is stated the practice works satisfactorily. The offences were:—

For using lights, gaff, or spear, .	36
For disturbing spawning fish, . . .	11
For having fish in possession during close season, . .	1
For assaulting bailiffs, ...	3
For minor offences, ...	4

Of these there were convictions in 36 cases, dismissals in 10, and the remainder were either withdrawn or adjourned.

There were 3 cases prosecuted by the Constabulary, and no returns of prosecutions by the Coast-guard has been received.

According to the accounts received the total expenditure for the year for water bailiffs £270, and for salaries £15. No expenses incurred for prosecutions, travelling, or miscellaneous expenses.

The revenue of the district for the year was derived from licence duties on 86 rods, 5 cross lines, 35 draft nets, 18 drift nets, 5 bag nets, 7 boxes or cribs, and 19 gaps or eyes for taking eels; amounting to £396.

	£	s.	d.
To which is to be added, . . .	396	0	0
Amount of fines received, . . .	1	6	8
And contribution from Sir C. Knox Gore, .	5	0	0
Total, .	402	6	8

In reply to the several queries as to the migration of salmon, grilse, and fry, the Conservators do not give any information. Grilse is first taken in middle of May, and the largest quantity in middle of June. In the middle of May and beginning of June salmon are taken with the grilse, and they are, as a rule, lighter than those taken in the early part of the season. The greatest quantity of salmon is taken in April and beginning of May.

The Conservators consider that the use of cross lines should be prohibited.

No. 12, or Sligo District,

Extends from Coonamore Point, County Sligo, to Mullaghmore Point, and includes that part of the country the waters of which flow into the coast between those two points.

Close Seasons.

The close seasons in force are—for tidal and fresh waters:—

"Between 19th August and 4th February, save Sligo river and Estuary, which is between 31st July and 16th January."

For angling with single rod—

"Between 30th September and 1st February, save in Drumcliffe river and Glencar lake between 15th October and 1st February; and in Grange River between 31st October and 1st February."

By-laws.

"Prohibiting the snatching, or attempting to snatch, salmon in Sligo river with any kind of fish-hook, covered in part or in whole, or uncovered.

"Permitting use of nets with meshes of half an inch from knot to knot, for capture of fish in Lough Dona."

The principal rivers in the Sligo district and the seasons for netting and angling for salmon or trout are as follows:—

Rivers.	Tidal Netting.	Freshwater Netting.	Angling with Single Rod and Line.
Ballisodare,	4th Feb. to 19th Aug. inclusive,	Same as Tidal,	1st Feb. to 30th Sept. inclusive,
Drumcliffe,	do.	do.	1st Feb. to 15th Oct. do.
Grange,	do.	do.	1st Feb. to 31st Oct. do.
Sligo,	16th Jan. to 31st July inclusive,	do.	1st Feb. to 30th Sept. do.

The state of the fisheries is reported good though the take was not so productive as 1884. The quantity of breeding fish was much greater than in preceding year. No sign of disease has been observed. No destruction of fry or spent fish. No poisoning. Offences have increased, but not yet prosecuted.

During the year there were no prosecutions in the district, by either the Conservators, Constabulary, or Coast Guard.

None of the Proprietors in the upper waters contribute funds for protection.

There are four bailiffs employed by the Conservators.

The expenditure, according to the accounts received, was:—

	£	s.	d.
For Bailiffs,	48	10	0
" Salaries,	15	18	0
" Prosecution Expenses,	2	0	0
" Postage and Printing,	3	7	6
Total,	69	15	6

The Revenue of the district was derived from Licenses sold:—21 rods; 20 draft nets; 1 bag net; and 7 gaps or eyes for taking eels, which amounted to £98, to which is to be added, Fines, 14s. 6d. Total, £98 14s. 6d.

To the special queries the Conservators reply that only one migration of smolts has been observed; that grilse is first taken in May, and the greatest quantity in July; that in June and July salmon are taken with the grilse, and are heavier than at other periods. The largest quantities of salmon are captured in January in the Sligo river, in April in Drumcliffe, and in April, May, and June, in Ballisodare.

The proportion of grilse taken to salmon is as six to one. Distinct runs of salmon in Sligo river have been observed in January, April, and November. In the Ballisodare river in May, June, and July, and in Drumcliffe in April, May, June, and July.

Concluding Observations.

On nearly the whole of the West of Ireland the take of salmon in 1885 was considerably more productive than 1884, and from every locality it is reported that a much larger quantity of breeding salmon was observed.

Some alterations in the law, recommended in former reports, which would be desirable, might be adopted, and would, in my mind, promote a greater interest in the people to protect the fish from many destructive practices.

THOS. F. BRADY

MAJOR HAYES' REPORT.

Division extending from Slea Head, in the County of Kerry in the west to Wicklow Head in the east, and including eight fishery districts—viz., No. 7, Killarney; No. 8', Kenmare; No. 6', Bantry; No. 6, Skibbereen; No. 5, Cork; No. 4, Lismore; No. 3, Waterford; and No. 2, Wexford, which embrace the whole or portions of the following counties, viz.:—Kerry, Cork, Waterford, Tipperary, Limerick, Kilkenny, Carlow, Wexford, Queen's County, King's County, Kildare, and Wicklow.

No. 8', Kenmare District.

Extending from Crow Head to Lamb Head, in the County of Kerry.

The capture of salmon in the Kenmare District was greater in 1885 than in the previous year, but it is reported that the peals and grilse were larger in the year 1884.

Fewer breeding fish are reported as in the spawning beds than in previous years—the decrease is attributed to continual poaching. This may be easily inferred from the fact that no less than thirteen cases of poisoning occurred during the year—one with lime and twelve cases by spurge.

The prices obtained for salmon were 8½d. to 1s. per lb.

Fifteen persons were summoned for offences against the fishery laws, at the instance of the Board of Conservators. Thirteen were convicted and fined, and in the remaining two the cases were dismissed.

In nine cases summonses were issued on the part of the Constabulary. In six the persons charged were convicted and fined; in the remaining three the cases failed.

Fifteen water bailiffs were employed by the Board of Conservators, and [illegible] others by private individuals, to protect their proprietary fisheries.

For the bye-laws in force in the district see p. 80, and for close season see p. 72.

During the season 1885 the following engines were licensed for fishing in the district:

30 Single rods.	3 Bag nets, and
6 Draft nets.	4 Snap nets.

The amount received was:—For licences, £81; for fines, £13 5s. 4d., less by £6 [illegible] moiety of penalties paid to prosecutors, and £10 received on account of percentage from proprietors of fisheries. The amount actually available for protection was £88 13s. 7d., an increase of £3 1s. 5d. on the receipts of 1884.

Artificial propagation of salmon is still successfully carried on in the river Blackwater by the proprietor, Richard Mahony, Esq., D.L., of Dromore Castle, about 80,000 ova having been hatched in 1885.

No. 6', Bantry District.

Extending from Crow Head to Mizen Head.

The season 1885 was a productive fishery year as far as the Bantry District was concerned.

The price obtained was 7d. per lb., and the average weight of the fish 5 to 6 lbs.

No signs of salmon disease have been perceived.

Poisoning, I regret to say, still continues, and during the season the Coomhola or Snave, the Ballylicky and Ouvane or Dorus rivers were poisoned with spurge.

Offences against the fishery laws are reported to have increased.

Three prosecutions were instituted on the part of the Conservators, and in each case successfully. In one case imprisonment for fourteen days followed the conviction for taking poisoned fish, and in the other two fines of £1 was awarded for spearing salmon.

The following licences to fish were issued by the Conservators:—14 single rods, 3 draft nets, 1 draft net.

The amount received and available for protection was—for licences, £42 10s., with £4 added, received for fines.

The amount expended in water-keeping was during the open season, £9 7s.; during close season, £30 16s., by the Board of Conservators. These sums represent the expenditure on water-keeping by the Board in addition to two bailiffs employed by the Earl of Bantry.

No. 6¹. Skibbereen District.

Extending from Galley Head to Mizen Head, in the County of Cork.

The take of salmon in this district and the stock of spawning fish were reported as less than in the previous year.

It is reported that offences against the Fishery Laws have diminished, **but several** cases of poisoning occurred during the season.

The price realised for salmon varied from 6d. to 8d. per lb.

For tables of close season and by-laws in force, see pp. 62 and 72 of Appendix.

There was only one prosecution for violation of the Fishery Laws during the season. The offender was convicted and fined in a sum of £2.

Five water-bailiffs were employed, at a total amount of £38 14s., the wages being from 3s. to 12s. 6d. per week.

The following engines were licensed for fishing during 1885:—Single rods, 4; draft nets, 13, producing a sum of £43, which, with £11 3s. 8d. received for fines, and 8s. interest on Bank account, produced £54 11s. 8d., available for protection.

No. 6. Cork District.

Extending from Ballycotton to Galley Head.

The capture by nets during season 1885 was in excess of that for 1884, and the season was considered fairly good. Rod fishing was not so good as during the previous year, the fish being unable to ascend to the angling waters during a portion of the season from the lowness of the water.

The spawning beds are reported as having been well stocked, although not so abundantly as in the previous year, owing to the same cause. At this date (24th January) it is reported that the tideway is still crowded with spawning fish, waiting to ascend the rivers.

The price of salmon varied from 6d. to 1s. 6d. per lb. **Salmon averaged 9 to 10 lbs.** in weight. The grilse were small—4 to 4½ lbs.

A few salmon, it is reported, were affected by the disease which caused such destruction in the Scotch rivers; but happily the disease appeared to be confined to fish which had recently spawned—few, if any, spring salmon or grilse were at all affected.

I have again to remark upon the great destruction of fish caused by poison, by means of a plant called spurge. The Sullane, an important spawning river, was poisoned no less than three times during the year, and the Upper Lee twice.

It is exceedingly difficult to secure convictions for this offence against the actual perpetrators, and the offence is one of the most destructive character, and requires to be dealt with in the most severe manner. But, as in general, other parties besides the principal offenders are engaged indirectly in this illegal work, who look out to take the poisoned fish, it is possible occasionally to obtain convictions against them, as by the 35th sec., 10 and 11 Vic., c. 92, it is enacted that—"Any person found taking fish from any river or lake where it shall be found to the satisfaction of the Justice or Justices that such fish have been wilfully poisoned, shall be subject to a penalty of not less than 10s., nor more than £5."

During the past year twelve persons were prosecuted for the offence of taking poisoned fish; convictions were had in eight cases, and penalties awarded of four or five pounds in most cases, with ten shillings costs. In four the prosecution failed.

Besides the above, forty-seven persons were prosecuted for breaches of the ordinary Fishery Laws at the instance of the Board of Conservators, twenty-seven were convicted, ten acquitted, and in ten cases the prosecutions (which were instituted for non-payment of licence duty) were withdrawn upon the parties paying their licences.

There were only two prosecutions by the Constabulary in all of which convictions followed, and fines of four pounds in each case inflicted.

Four persons were summoned by the Coast Guard, but in all the cases acquittals followed.

During the winter season from 1st October to 1st February, six water bailiffs were constantly employed to protect the tidal waters and ten on the upper or fresh water portion of the river; and from 1st February to 1st October, seven in the tidal, and fifteen on the upper or fresh waters.

The total expenditure on water bailiffs amounted to £255 1s. 10d. The purposes protection, [illegible] the greatest expenditure, in consequence of the persistent poaching prevailing in the tidal waters.

For Tables of bye-laws and close seasons in force in the district, see pages 63, 72, in the Appendix.

During the year we held public enquiries at Bandon and Inishannon, into the necessity or expediency of continuing the bye-law made in 1878, which prohibited net fishing in the Bandon River for a period of five years above a line drawn across the river at right angles with the stream course, from the stream dividing the townlands of [illegible] and [illegible], to the stream on the opposite shore dividing the townlands of [illegible] and [illegible]. We came to the conclusion that a more extended area might be given to the net fishermen, and we accordingly made a bye-law on the 6th July, 1885, and which was approved by the Lord Lieutenant in Council on the 5th of March, by which the boundary above which no net fishing should take place was fixed at a line drawn across the river at right angles to the river's course from the stream on the east side of the river dividing the townlands of [illegible] and [illegible], in a westerly direction to the opposite shore. The following is a copy of the bye-law.

Bye-law.

[illegible]

"Each and every person offending against this bye-law, shall forfeit and pay for each offence a sum of five pounds, and any net or other engine used in committing such offence shall be forfeited."

This bye-law extends the area by about half a mile of valuable netting ground.

The licences issued during 1885 were, for the Cork Division, 101 single salmon rods, 43 draft nets, 1 bag-net, and 1 [illegible] weir—the money value amounting to £375, to which must be added £35 11s. 5d. received for fines, £8 realized by the sale of forfeited engines, and £75 subscriptions, in all £531 11s. 5d., available for protection of River Lee and tributaries.

The licences issued for the Bandon division were 120 single rods, 2 cross lines, 20 draft nets, producing £263, to which must be added £25 8s. 10d. received for fines, and £1 on sale of forfeited engines, total £289 8s. 10d.

The total revenue from the entire district was therefore £788 0s. 4d.

No. 4, Lismore District.

Extending from Ballycotton, county Cork, to Helvick Head, in the county of Waterford.

The season 1885 was a most productive one in the Lismore district—it is believed that it was the best for the last fourteen years—the fishing in the district in a great measure depends upon the prevailing winds during the fishing season, and it is stated that west and southerly winds, which are the most suitable, prevailed to a great extent.

The quantity of breeding fish in the spawning beds was about the usual average.

Average weight of salmon, 11 to 12 lbs.; peale 1 to 5 lbs.

Up to 13th June the price varied from 1s. 2d. to 1s. 8d. per lb.; from middle of June to 10th August it varied from 8d. to 10d.

There were 70 prosecutions for fishery offences at the instance of the Board of Conservators, in all of which the offenders were convicted, and fined in amounts varying from 10s. to £5.

Twenty-five persons were prosecuted by the Constabulary, and in all cases convictions followed, the fines varying from 10s. to £4.

Thirty-one water bailiffs were employed by the Conservators from the 1st October, 1884, to 1st February, 1885; and fifteen from 1st February to 1st October following—involving an expenditure of £[illegible] during the open season, and £[illegible] during the close season.

For tables of close seasons and copies of bye-laws in force in this district, see pp. [illegible] of Appendix.

The following engines were licensed to fish during the season 1885:—single salmon rods, [illegible]; cross lines, [illegible]; snap nets, [illegible]; draft nets or seines, 17; drift nets, 68; pole nets, [illegible]; bag nets, [illegible]; stake nets, [illegible]; boxes or cribs, [illegible].

The above produced £[illegible]—to this sum to be added for fines and costs, £83 12s. 4d.; sale of forfeited engines, £[illegible]; subscriptions, £[illegible], and £[illegible] amount received upon the 10 per cent. Poor Law Valuation of several fisheries.

The total amount received and available for protection amounted to £[illegible] 0s. 4d.

No. 3, or Waterford District.

Extending from Helvick Head, in the county of Waterford, to Kiln Bay (east of Bannow Bay), in the county of Wexford.

The general state of the salmon fisheries of the Waterford district for 1885 is reported as having been very satisfactory. The take of fish was much about the same as in 1884, but it is believed that it would have been greater but for the dry summer, and the absence of south-west winds during the fishing season—the want of these winds always operating against the capture of fish in the tideways.

The same remarks apply to the capture of fish in the year 1884, which was affected by the same cause.

The breeding rivers were well stocked with spawning fish.

The rentals for rod fisheries are reported as having decreased in consequence of the disturbed state of the country.

No appearance of salmon disease has been observed in the district during 1885.

Offences against the fishery laws were reported to have greatly decreased, and this is attributed to more efficient protection. There were [illegible] persons prosecuted at the instance of the Board of Conservators—[illegible] of these were convicted and fined, and in [illegible] cases [illegible] followed. [illegible] persons were summoned by the Constabulary, resulting in [illegible] convictions, [illegible] acquittals, and in 2 cases the prosecutions were withdrawn, so that there were less in the last year by [illegible], as compared with the year 1884. The fines varied from [illegible] to £[illegible].

There were no prosecutions by the Coast Guard.

A very large staff of water bailiffs were employed throughout the district, both in the open and close seasons. In the open season, from 1st February to 1st October, a period of eight months, about £[illegible] was expended in payments, and during close season, from 1st October to 1st February, only three months, £[illegible].

The following licences for fishing were issued in 1885, [illegible] single salmon rods, [illegible] cross lines, [illegible] snap nets, 34 draft nets, 87 drift nets, 1 bag net, 4 stake weirs, 4 boxes or cribs, 27 licences for [illegible]; these produced a sum of £[illegible]. To this sum is to be added £[illegible], received for fines, [illegible] produced by sale of forfeited engines, £[illegible], 10 per cent. upon valuation of several fisheries, £[illegible], interest on bank accounts, and £[illegible] subscriptions, producing altogether a sum amounting to £[illegible] 17s. [illegible] available for protection.

The following important bye-laws, made during the year, having been approved by the Lord Lieutenant and Privy Council, are now in force in this district.

Bye-laws.

"Whereas the practice of [illegible] for the purpose of [illegible] fish [illegible] on the banks of the rivers in the district [illegible] known as No. 3, or Waterford District, in the counties of Waterford, Wexford, Kildare, Carlow, Kilkenny, King's, Queen's, Tipperary, and Limerick, which comprises the [illegible] Helvick Head, in the county of Waterford, and Kiln Bay, in the county of Wexford, is [illegible] detrimental to the fisheries, and it seems fit to us, the Inspectors of Irish Fisheries, to be expedient for the more effectual government, management, protection, and improvement of the salmon and trout fisheries in the said district, to prohibit such practices. Now, we, the said Inspectors, [illegible] do make and ordain this bye-law, by which it is prohibited, and it is hereby prohibited [illegible] or other missiles thereon, for the purpose of driving fish [illegible] within the said district.

"Each and every person offending against this bye-law shall forfeit and pay for each offence a sum of Two Pounds."

"Whereas it seems fit to us, the Inspectors of Irish Fisheries, to be expedient for the more effectual government, management, protection, and improvement of the salmon and trout fisheries in the Waterford District, that all boats engaged in fishing for salmon or trout should be distinctly marked [illegible]. Now we, the pursuance of the powers and authorities in us vested by the abovenamed Acts, do make and ordain the following by-laws, rules, and regulations to be observed by all persons engaged in fishing for or taking salmon or trout in the Wexford District.—

1st.—“Each and every boat used in salmon and trout fishing shall have marked on each bow, with distinct figures of not less than six inches in length and one inch in breadth, a number corresponding with the number on the license issued for the net used with such boat.

2nd.—“The said numbers shall be painted in white oil colour on a black ground.

3rd.—“The numbers so placed on boats shall not be effaced, covered, or concealed in any manner whatsoever.

“Any person offending against any of these by-laws, rules, and regulations, shall forfeit and pay for each offence a sum of Two Pounds.”

“Whereas [illegible]

“[illegible]”

“Whereas [illegible]

“[illegible]”

For bye-laws and close seasons in force in the District, see pp. 67 and 72.

No. 2.—Wexford District.

Extending from Wicklow Head, in the County of Wicklow, to Kiln Bay, east of Barrow Bay, in the County of Wexford.

The condition of the fisheries in the Wexford district was reported to be much the same as during the previous year, but the stock of breeding fish on the spawning grounds as greater than for any year during the last ten.

The size of the salmon was about the same as the preceding year, the average weight being salmon, 10 lbs., peale 5 lbs.

The prices obtained were from 6d. to 1s. 6d. per lb.

It is much to be regretted that the salmon disease appeared in the district, and many fish died from its effects; it is roughly calculated that about £200 worth of fish so perished.

The capture of salmon and peale were nearly equal, perhaps the salmon may have been slightly greater.

Offences against the fishery laws are reported to have diminished, and this is attributed to more efficient watching than formerly.

There were 15 prosecutions for fishery offences on the part of the Board of Conservators, of these ten were convicted and fined, and in five the cases were dismissed. The fines varied from 10s. to £5.

Two persons were prosecuted by the Constabulary, and in each case the parties were convicted.

The amount expended upon water keeping was £283 4s. 6d., viz., £210 18s. 6d., during the close season, and £73 6s. during the open season; of this £69 6s. was expended in protecting the lower or tidal waters.

During the season 1885 the following engines were licensed for fishing—

104 Single rods.
80 Draft nets.

The licences produced £344, this with interest allowed on the bank balances, £3 9s. 8d., and £30 8s. 7d. received for fines, produced a revenue of £377 18s. 3d. available for protection.

For bye-laws and close seasons in force in the District, see pp. 67, 78, Appendix.

No. 7. Killarney District.

Extending from Lamb Head to Dunmore Head, both in the County of Kerry.

The state of the fisheries in this District during 1885, was most satisfactory. The previous year was regarded as a productive one, but the past year was considerably better, each month showing an increase as compared with the corresponding month of 1884.

The quantity of breeding fish is reported as having been very large, but owing to the scarcity of water in the small rivers, the fish principally spawned in the larger ones.

The prices realised were much the same as in 1884—viz., 2s. 6d. per lb. in February, and 1s. 6d. in March, but in July it fell to 5d.

The average size of the fish almost the same as in 1884—viz., spring salmon, 11 lbs., grilse, 6½ lbs.

Twenty-four persons were summoned at the instance of the Board of Conservators for offences against the fishery laws. In eighteen convictions followed, and penalties awarded varying from 10s. to £5 in each case. In the remaining six, the cases were dismissed.

Five persons were prosecuted by the Constabulary, and convictions were had in each—the fines varied from 10s. to 20s. each.

Sixty-seven water bailiffs were employed—those in the spawning rivers from October to March. In the open season the expenditure amounted to £91, in the close season to £165.

The bailiffs permanently employed received from £5 to £8 each for the season. Those specially employed for the protection of the spawning rivers, from £4 to £14 each.

There have not been any special contributions in aid of the funds for general protection, but private bailiffs have been employed by the Hon. Rowland Winn, James Butler, esq., R. H. Hartropp, esq., G. M'Gillicuddy Eagar, esq., and Messrs. Power and Dodd.

Only one case of poisoning occurred in this district during 1885. This was in the river Flesk. The parties were caught on the bank of the river at night by the Constabulary, when a cartload of lime had been thrown in. The parties were prosecuted at Killarney Petty Sessions, and three of them were fined £5 each. On appeal, the Chairman of Quarter Sessions reversed the convictions, as the parties were not actually seen putting the lime into the river.

The following licenses were issued during the year:—90 single rods; 5 cross lines; 6 draft nets, and 2 boxes. The licenses produced the sum of £300, added to which £30 10s. for fines, £1 5s. received for sale of forfeited engine, and £27 8s. ten per cent. upon the Poor Law Valuation—made a gross total of £359 3s. available for protection.

For tables of close seasons and bye-laws in force in the District, see pp. 69 and 79 of Appendix.

Concluding Observations.

That the Salmon Fisheries of Ireland are steadily improving may safely be inferred from the following table, showing the number of persons employed in the capture of salmon, the number of the various engines used for the purpose, and the amounts paid annually for the License duty from 1863 to the year 1885. It will be seen by reference to this table that there has been a steady increase in the number of men and engines, and also in the revenue derived therefrom. It cannot be supposed that increased numbers would embark in fishing enterprise or pay increased licence duty unless they obtained fair remuneration for their trouble and outlay.

Years.	[illegible]	Single Rods	Draft Nets	Drift Nets	Bag Nets	Stake Weirs	Head Weirs	Box, &c.	No. of Men	Amount.
										£
1868,	[illegible]	[illegible]	[illegible]	[illegible]	[illegible]	[illegible]	[illegible]	14	[illegible]	7,0[illegible]
1869,	[illegible]	[illegible]	[illegible]	[illegible]	[illegible]	[illegible]	[illegible]	68	[illegible]	8,440
1870,	[illegible]	[illegible]	[illegible]	[illegible]	[illegible]	[illegible]	[illegible]	35	[illegible]	7,811
1871,	[illegible]	[illegible]	[illegible]	[illegible]	[illegible]	[illegible]	[illegible]	65	[illegible]	8,865
1872,	[illegible]	[illegible]	[illegible]	[illegible]	[illegible]	[illegible]	[illegible]	38	10,250	8,369
1873,	[illegible]	[illegible]	[illegible]	[illegible]	[illegible]	[illegible]	[illegible]	85	[illegible]	8,040
1874,	[illegible]	[illegible]	[illegible]	[illegible]	[illegible]	[illegible]	[illegible]	[illegible]	[illegible]	9,115
1875,	[illegible]	[illegible]	[illegible]	[illegible]	[illegible]	[illegible]	[illegible]	85	[illegible]	10,949
1876,	[illegible]	[illegible]	[illegible]	[illegible]	[illegible]	[illegible]	[illegible]	44	[illegible]	10,644
1877,	[illegible]	[illegible]	[illegible]	[illegible]	[illegible]	[illegible]	[illegible]	45	[illegible]	[illegible]
1878,	[illegible]	[illegible]	[illegible]	[illegible]	[illegible]	[illegible]	[illegible]	44	[illegible]	[illegible]
1879,	[illegible]	[illegible]	[illegible]	[illegible]	[illegible]	[illegible]	[illegible]	[illegible]	[illegible]	[illegible]
1880,	[illegible]	[illegible]	[illegible]	[illegible]	[illegible]	[illegible]	1	[illegible]	[illegible]	[illegible]
1881,	[illegible]	[illegible]	[illegible]	[illegible]	[illegible]	[illegible]	[illegible]	41	[illegible]	[illegible]
1882,	[illegible]	[illegible]	[illegible]	[illegible]	[illegible]	[illegible]	[illegible]	32	[illegible]	[illegible]
1883,	[illegible]	[illegible]	[illegible]	[illegible]	[illegible]	[illegible]	[illegible]	45	[illegible]	11,970
1884,	[illegible]	[illegible]	[illegible]	[illegible]	[illegible]	[illegible]	[illegible]	[illegible]	[illegible]	13,180
1885,	[illegible]	[illegible]	[illegible]	32	[illegible]	[illegible]	1	36	[illegible]	13,915

A certain amount of illegal fishing may always be expected to take place, as when there is an abundance of fish the temptation to the poacher is greater than he can resist; but a system of the most destructive nature has been steadily growing, especially in the South, which is most difficult to deal with, and which, if not checked, will, I fear, inflict very serious injury to the salmon fisheries.

I mean the wholesale poisoning of fish. Last year there were several cases in the County of Cork, and it is alleged that very large quantities of fish were destroyed thereby.

Lime or a weed called spurge (euphorbia hybernica) are used, and the misfortune is that they not only kill the mature and marketable fish, but that everything possessing life in the way of fish is killed.

It is alleged that the fry of salmon and trout have been destroyed by it in great quantities, and if continued this must without doubt materially affect the future of our salmon fisheries most injuriously. I trust means may be found in some way to render the trade of the poacher more precarious and uncertain than it has hitherto been, and I am not without hope that means will be discovered which will effectually put a stop to the practice.

I beg to refer to the concluding observations of my report for 1884 with reference to amendment of the Fishery Laws, which I beg to reiterate.

JOS. HAYES.

Having given in the foregoing Report all the detailed information in our power, we have only to add that we have at all times experienced the most cordial co-operation from the officers and men of Her Majesty's Coast Guard and the Royal Irish Constabulary authorities in enforcing the laws, and to them our best thanks are due.

We have the honour to be,

Your Excellency's very obedient servants,

THOMAS F. BRADY.
JOS. HAYES.
ALAN HORNSBY.

GEORGE COFFEY, Secretary.

Dated at the Fisheries Office, Dublin Castle,
17th June, 1886.

APPENDIX.

APPENDIX No. 1.—ABSTRACT of RETURNS from COAST-GUARD of the NUMBERS of VESSELS, BOATS, and CREWS, engaged in the SEA FISHERIES in 1888.

No.	Name of Division.	Registering Officer.	Wholly engaged in Fishing: First Class: Vessels	Men	Boys	Second Class: Vessels	Men	Boys	Third Class: Vessels	Men	Boys	Only partially employed in Fishing: First Class: Vessels	Men	Boys	Second Class: Vessels	Men	Boys	Third Class: Vessels	Men	Boys	Totals: Vessels	Men	Boys	No.
1	[illegible]	[illegible]	[illegible]	[illegible]	[illegible]	[illegible]	[illegible]	[illegible]	[illegible]	[illegible]	[illegible]	[illegible]	[illegible]	[illegible]	[illegible]	[illegible]	[illegible]	[illegible]	[illegible]	[illegible]	[illegible]	[illegible]	[illegible]	1
2	Arklow,	[illegible]	[illegible]	[illegible]	[illegible]	[illegible]	[illegible]	[illegible]	[illegible]	[illegible]	[illegible]	[illegible]	[illegible]	[illegible]	[illegible]	[illegible]	[illegible]	[illegible]	[illegible]	[illegible]	[illegible]	[illegible]	[illegible]	2
3	Wexford,	[illegible]	[illegible]	[illegible]	[illegible]	[illegible]	[illegible]	[illegible]	[illegible]	[illegible]	[illegible]	[illegible]	[illegible]	[illegible]	[illegible]	[illegible]	[illegible]	[illegible]	[illegible]	[illegible]	[illegible]	[illegible]	[illegible]	3
4	Waterford,	[illegible]	[illegible]	[illegible]	[illegible]	[illegible]	[illegible]	[illegible]	[illegible]	[illegible]	[illegible]	[illegible]	[illegible]	[illegible]	[illegible]	[illegible]	[illegible]	[illegible]	[illegible]	[illegible]	[illegible]	[illegible]	[illegible]	4
5	Youghal,	[illegible]	[illegible]	[illegible]	[illegible]	[illegible]	[illegible]	[illegible]	[illegible]	[illegible]	[illegible]	[illegible]	[illegible]	[illegible]	[illegible]	[illegible]	[illegible]	[illegible]	[illegible]	[illegible]	[illegible]	[illegible]	[illegible]	5
6	Queenstown,	[illegible]	[illegible]	[illegible]	[illegible]	[illegible]	[illegible]	[illegible]	[illegible]	[illegible]	[illegible]	[illegible]	[illegible]	[illegible]	[illegible]	[illegible]	[illegible]	[illegible]	[illegible]	[illegible]	[illegible]	[illegible]	[illegible]	6
7	Kinsale,	[illegible]	[illegible]	[illegible]	[illegible]	[illegible]	[illegible]	[illegible]	[illegible]	[illegible]	[illegible]	[illegible]	[illegible]	[illegible]	[illegible]	[illegible]	[illegible]	[illegible]	[illegible]	[illegible]	[illegible]	[illegible]	[illegible]	7
8	[illegible]	[illegible]	[illegible]	[illegible]	[illegible]	[illegible]	[illegible]	[illegible]	[illegible]	[illegible]	[illegible]	[illegible]	[illegible]	[illegible]	[illegible]	[illegible]	[illegible]	[illegible]	[illegible]	[illegible]	[illegible]	[illegible]	[illegible]	8
9	[illegible]	[illegible]	[illegible]	[illegible]	[illegible]	[illegible]	[illegible]	[illegible]	[illegible]	[illegible]	[illegible]	[illegible]	[illegible]	[illegible]	[illegible]	[illegible]	[illegible]	[illegible]	[illegible]	[illegible]	[illegible]	[illegible]	[illegible]	9
10	[illegible]	[illegible]	[illegible]	[illegible]	[illegible]	[illegible]	[illegible]	[illegible]	[illegible]	[illegible]	[illegible]	[illegible]	[illegible]	[illegible]	[illegible]	[illegible]	[illegible]	[illegible]	[illegible]	[illegible]	[illegible]	[illegible]	[illegible]	10
11	[illegible]	[illegible]	[illegible]	[illegible]	[illegible]	[illegible]	[illegible]	[illegible]	[illegible]	[illegible]	[illegible]	[illegible]	[illegible]	[illegible]	[illegible]	[illegible]	[illegible]	[illegible]	[illegible]	[illegible]	[illegible]	[illegible]	[illegible]	11
12	[illegible]	[illegible]	[illegible]	[illegible]	[illegible]	[illegible]	[illegible]	[illegible]	[illegible]	[illegible]	[illegible]	[illegible]	[illegible]	[illegible]	[illegible]	[illegible]	[illegible]	[illegible]	[illegible]	[illegible]	[illegible]	[illegible]	[illegible]	12
13	[illegible]	[illegible]	[illegible]	[illegible]	[illegible]	[illegible]	[illegible]	[illegible]	[illegible]	[illegible]	[illegible]	[illegible]	[illegible]	[illegible]	[illegible]	[illegible]	[illegible]	[illegible]	[illegible]	[illegible]	[illegible]	[illegible]	[illegible]	13
14	Galway,	[illegible]	[illegible]	[illegible]	[illegible]	[illegible]	[illegible]	[illegible]	[illegible]	[illegible]	[illegible]	[illegible]	[illegible]	[illegible]	[illegible]	[illegible]	[illegible]	[illegible]	[illegible]	[illegible]	[illegible]	[illegible]	[illegible]	14
15	Clifden,	[illegible]	[illegible]	[illegible]	[illegible]	[illegible]	[illegible]	[illegible]	[illegible]	[illegible]	[illegible]	[illegible]	[illegible]	[illegible]	[illegible]	[illegible]	[illegible]	[illegible]	[illegible]	[illegible]	[illegible]	[illegible]	[illegible]	15
16	Keel,	[illegible]	[illegible]	[illegible]	[illegible]	[illegible]	[illegible]	[illegible]	[illegible]	[illegible]	[illegible]	[illegible]	[illegible]	[illegible]	[illegible]	[illegible]	[illegible]	[illegible]	[illegible]	[illegible]	[illegible]	[illegible]	[illegible]	16
17	[illegible]	[illegible]	[illegible]	[illegible]	[illegible]	[illegible]	[illegible]	[illegible]	[illegible]	[illegible]	[illegible]	[illegible]	[illegible]	[illegible]	[illegible]	[illegible]	[illegible]	[illegible]	[illegible]	[illegible]	[illegible]	[illegible]	[illegible]	17
18	[illegible]	[illegible]	[illegible]	[illegible]	[illegible]	[illegible]	[illegible]	[illegible]	[illegible]	[illegible]	[illegible]	[illegible]	[illegible]	[illegible]	[illegible]	[illegible]	[illegible]	[illegible]	[illegible]	[illegible]	[illegible]	[illegible]	[illegible]	18
19	[illegible]	[illegible]	[illegible]	[illegible]	[illegible]	[illegible]	[illegible]	[illegible]	[illegible]	[illegible]	[illegible]	[illegible]	[illegible]	[illegible]	[illegible]	[illegible]	[illegible]	[illegible]	[illegible]	[illegible]	[illegible]	[illegible]	[illegible]	19
20	[illegible]	[illegible]	[illegible]	[illegible]	[illegible]	[illegible]	[illegible]	[illegible]	[illegible]	[illegible]	[illegible]	[illegible]	[illegible]	[illegible]	[illegible]	[illegible]	[illegible]	[illegible]	[illegible]	[illegible]	[illegible]	[illegible]	[illegible]	20
21	[illegible]	[illegible]	[illegible]	[illegible]	[illegible]	[illegible]	[illegible]	[illegible]	[illegible]	[illegible]	[illegible]	[illegible]	[illegible]	[illegible]	[illegible]	[illegible]	[illegible]	[illegible]	[illegible]	[illegible]	[illegible]	[illegible]	[illegible]	21
22	[illegible]	[illegible]	[illegible]	[illegible]	[illegible]	[illegible]	[illegible]	[illegible]	[illegible]	[illegible]	[illegible]	[illegible]	[illegible]	[illegible]	[illegible]	[illegible]	[illegible]	[illegible]	[illegible]	[illegible]	[illegible]	[illegible]	[illegible]	22
23	[illegible]	[illegible]	[illegible]	[illegible]	[illegible]	[illegible]	[illegible]	[illegible]	[illegible]	[illegible]	[illegible]	[illegible]	[illegible]	[illegible]	[illegible]	[illegible]	[illegible]	[illegible]	[illegible]	[illegible]	[illegible]	[illegible]	[illegible]	23
24	[illegible]	[illegible]	[illegible]	[illegible]	[illegible]	[illegible]	[illegible]	[illegible]	[illegible]	[illegible]	[illegible]	[illegible]	[illegible]	[illegible]	[illegible]	[illegible]	[illegible]	[illegible]	[illegible]	[illegible]	[illegible]	[illegible]	[illegible]	24
25	[illegible]	[illegible]	[illegible]	[illegible]	[illegible]	[illegible]	[illegible]	[illegible]	[illegible]	[illegible]	[illegible]	[illegible]	[illegible]	[illegible]	[illegible]	[illegible]	[illegible]	[illegible]	[illegible]	[illegible]	[illegible]	[illegible]	[illegible]	25
26	[illegible]	[illegible]	[illegible]	[illegible]	[illegible]	[illegible]	[illegible]	[illegible]	[illegible]	[illegible]	[illegible]	[illegible]	[illegible]	[illegible]	[illegible]	[illegible]	[illegible]	[illegible]	[illegible]	[illegible]	[illegible]	[illegible]	[illegible]	26
27	[illegible]	[illegible]	[illegible]	[illegible]	[illegible]	[illegible]	[illegible]	[illegible]	[illegible]	[illegible]	[illegible]	[illegible]	[illegible]	[illegible]	[illegible]	[illegible]	[illegible]	[illegible]	[illegible]	[illegible]	[illegible]	[illegible]	[illegible]	27
28	[illegible]	[illegible]	[illegible]	[illegible]	[illegible]	[illegible]	[illegible]	[illegible]	[illegible]	[illegible]	[illegible]	[illegible]	[illegible]	[illegible]	[illegible]	[illegible]	[illegible]	[illegible]	[illegible]	[illegible]	[illegible]	[illegible]	[illegible]	28
29	[illegible]	[illegible]	[illegible]	[illegible]	[illegible]	[illegible]	[illegible]	[illegible]	[illegible]	[illegible]	[illegible]	[illegible]	[illegible]	[illegible]	[illegible]	[illegible]	[illegible]	[illegible]	[illegible]	[illegible]	[illegible]	[illegible]	[illegible]	29
30	[illegible]	[illegible]	[illegible]	[illegible]	[illegible]	[illegible]	[illegible]	[illegible]	[illegible]	[illegible]	[illegible]	[illegible]	[illegible]	[illegible]	[illegible]	[illegible]	[illegible]	[illegible]	[illegible]	[illegible]	[illegible]	[illegible]	[illegible]	30
31	[illegible]	[illegible]	[illegible]	[illegible]	[illegible]	[illegible]	[illegible]	[illegible]	[illegible]	[illegible]	[illegible]	[illegible]	[illegible]	[illegible]	[illegible]	[illegible]	[illegible]	[illegible]	[illegible]	[illegible]	[illegible]	[illegible]	[illegible]	31
32	[illegible]	[illegible]	[illegible]	[illegible]	[illegible]	[illegible]	[illegible]	[illegible]	[illegible]	[illegible]	[illegible]	[illegible]	[illegible]	[illegible]	[illegible]	[illegible]	[illegible]	[illegible]	[illegible]	[illegible]	[illegible]	[illegible]	[illegible]	32
		Total,	[illegible]	[illegible]	[illegible]	[illegible]	[illegible]	[illegible]	[illegible]	[illegible]	[illegible]	[illegible]	[illegible]	[illegible]	[illegible]	[illegible]	[illegible]	[illegible]	[illegible]	[illegible]	[illegible]	[illegible]	[illegible]	

APPENDIX No. 2.

ABSTRACT of BY-LAWS, ORDERS, &c., in force on 1st January, 1886, relating to the *Sea and Oyster* FISHERIES of IRELAND.

[illegible]	[illegible]	[illegible]	Purport of By-Law.
	TRAWLING.		
[illegible]	[illegible]	[illegible]	[illegible]
[illegible]	[illegible]	[illegible]	[illegible]
1st Dec., 1879.	[illegible]	[illegible]	TRAMMEL NETS. [illegible]
[illegible]	[illegible]		
[illegible]	[illegible]		
[illegible]	[illegible]	[illegible]	[illegible]
[illegible]	[illegible]	[illegible]	[illegible]
[illegible]	[illegible]		
[illegible]	[illegible]		
[illegible]	[illegible]		
[illegible]	[illegible]	[illegible]	[illegible]
[illegible]	[illegible]		

Appendix No. 1—continued.

Abstract of By-Laws, ... relating to the Sea and Oyster Fisheries of Ireland.

APPENDIX, No. 1—continued.

Abstract of Bye-Laws, Orders, &c., in force on 1st January, 1888, relating to the Sea and Oyster Fisheries of Ireland.

APPENDIX No. 6—continued.

ABSTRACT of Bye-Laws, Orders, &c., in force on 1st January, [illegible], relating to the Sea and Oyster Fisheries of Ireland.

APPENDIX No. 2—continued.

[illegible] in force on 1st January, 1886, relating to the Sea and Oyster Fisheries of Ireland.

Nature of By-Law.	[illegible]	Substance of By-Law.
[illegible]	[illegible]	[illegible]

APPENDIX No. 7—continued.

ABSTRACT of BY-LAWS, ORDERS, &c., in force on 1st January, 1886, relating to the Sea and Oyster FISHERIES of IRELAND

Place affected by By-Law, and Date Passed	Nature of By-Law.	Place affected by By-Law, and Date Passed	Nature of By-Law.
CARLINGFORD LOUGH (21st June, 1877.)	Prohibiting at any time after the 1st day of September, 1877, [illegible]	CARLINGFORD LOUGH—continued.	[illegible]
(1st Aug., 1884.)	[illegible]		[illegible]
(15th Oct., 1884.)	First.—During the Close Time [illegible] Second.—[illegible]		Third,—[illegible]
		(6th May, 1885.)	Prohibiting to dredge for, take, [illegible]

APPENDIX No. 8.

LIST of OYSTER LICENSES REVOKED up to date of this Report.

Date of License.	Persons to whom granted.	Locality of Beds.	No. of Acres	Date of Revocation.
County Antrim.				
[illegible]. 3rd March,	James Walker,	Belfast Lough,	187	7th March, 1877.
County Cork.				
[illegible] 26th February,	R. T. Evanson,	Dunmanus Bay,	19	21st November, [illegible]
1867. 27th August,	Thomas Eccles,	Glengarriffe Harbour,	9	31st October, 1878.
[illegible]. 4th October,	M. C. Cramer,	Oyster Haven,	[illegible]	1st February, [illegible]
1864. 31st October,	R. T. Atkins,	Lough Hyne,	[illegible]	1st February, [illegible]
1867. 10th July,	M. J. C. Longfield,	Roaringwater Bay,	200	7th March, 1877.
1867. 10th July,	H. H. Townsend,	[illegible] Harbour,	[illegible]	28th April, 1884.
[illegible]. 12th March,	Stephen Brown,	Dunmanus Bay,	9	31st October, 1881
[illegible]. 25th February,	Earl of Bantry,	Adrigole Harbour,	10	9th March, 1878.
[illegible]. 12th March,	John Warren Payne,	Bantry Bay,	41	19th October, [illegible]
1871. 22nd March,	Earl of Bantry and T. J. Leahy,	Bearhaven,	[illegible]	12th March, 1878.
1873. 21st June,	Earl of Bandon,	Dunmanus Bay,	[illegible]	31st October, [illegible]
1874. 28th January,	Sir H. W. Becher,	Lough Hyne,	20	1st February, [illegible]

APPENDIX No. 3—continued.

LIST of OYSTER LICENSES [illegible] up to date of this Report—continued.

Date of License	Persons to whom granted	Locality of Beds	No. of Acres	Date of [illegible]
County Donegal.				
[illegible] 31st January,	William Hart,	Lough Swilly,	700	[illegible] February, 18[illegible]
18[illegible] 30th November,	John Alexander Doherty,	Lough Foyle,	97	[illegible] July, 18[illegible]
County Kerry.				
1865. 3rd February,	Knight of Kerry,	Valentia Harbour,	[illegible]	[illegible] March, 18[illegible]
1867. 10th July,	[illegible],	River Shannon,	700	[illegible] October, 18[illegible]
1868. 18th February,	[illegible],	Kenmare Bay,	103	[illegible] May, 18[illegible]
1871. 27th March,	Earl of [illegible],	[illegible] Harbour,	[illegible]	[illegible] December, 18[illegible]
County Galway.				
1864. 31st October,	R. H. Lynch Athy,	Galway Bay,	110	[illegible] March, 18[illegible]
1864. 31st October,	P. M. Lynch,	Do.,	[illegible]	[illegible] April, 18[illegible]
1864. 31st December,	T. Young Prior,	Ballynakill Harbour,	60	[illegible] June, 18[illegible]
1865. 1st December,	Captain [illegible],	Do.,	[illegible]	[illegible] April, 18[illegible]
1865. 1st December,	[illegible],	Killary Bay,	[illegible]	[illegible] April, 18[illegible]
1867. 10th July,	William and James [illegible],	Galway Bay,	600	[illegible] January, 18[illegible]
1867. 10th July,	Christopher T. Redington,	Do.,	600	[illegible] March, 18[illegible]
County Mayo.				
18[illegible] [illegible] November,	William Pike,	Achill Sound,	[illegible]	[illegible] September, 18[illegible]
18[illegible] [illegible] April,	Marquess of Sligo,	Clew Bay,	[illegible]	[illegible] October, 18[illegible]
18[illegible] 2nd November,	Law Life Assurance Society,	Do.,	[illegible]	[illegible] January, 18[illegible]
18[illegible] 1st December,	Marquess of Sligo,	Do.,	60	[illegible] October, 18[illegible]
18[illegible] [illegible] April,	Do.,	Do.,	[illegible]	[illegible] October, 18[illegible]
18[illegible] 10th July,	[illegible],	[illegible] Bay,	[illegible]	[illegible] June, 18[illegible]
18[illegible] 14th June,	William [illegible],	[illegible] Bay,	[illegible]	[illegible] October, 18[illegible]
18[illegible] 3rd July,	[illegible],	Blacksod Bay,	[illegible]	[illegible] April, 18[illegible]
18[illegible] 10th December,	William O. M'Cormick,	[illegible] Bay,	[illegible]	[illegible] January, 18[illegible]
18[illegible] 1st December,	[illegible] Whitney,	Blacksod Bay,	[illegible]	[illegible] April, 1881.
18[illegible] [illegible] December,	Mary Higgins,	Clew Bay,	[illegible]	[illegible] May, 18[illegible]
18[illegible] [illegible] December,	Owen Bingham,	Blacksod Bay,	[illegible]	[illegible] June, 18[illegible]
18[illegible] [illegible] October,	[illegible],	[illegible] Bay,	2	[illegible] July, 18[illegible]
County Sligo.				
1871. [illegible] April,	Edward [illegible],	[illegible],	[illegible]	[illegible] October, 18[illegible]
1871. [illegible] April,	[illegible],	Do.,	[illegible]	[illegible] October, 18[illegible]
1871. [illegible] April,	Michael [illegible],	Do.,	[illegible]	[illegible] October, 18[illegible]
1873. 3rd March,	[illegible] L. [illegible],	Do.,	[illegible]	[illegible] October, 18[illegible]
County Waterford.				
18[illegible] [illegible] November,	John [illegible],	[illegible] Harbour,	[illegible]	[illegible] March, 18[illegible]

List of Licenses to Plant Oysters [illegible] in force on 31st December [illegible]

[illegible]	[illegible]	[illegible]	[illegible]	[illegible]	[illegible]	[illegible]
	County [illegible]					
[illegible]	[illegible]	[illegible]	....	[illegible]	[illegible]	[illegible]
	County [illegible]					
[illegible]	[illegible]	[illegible]	[illegible]	[illegible]	[illegible]	
	County [illegible]					
[illegible]	[illegible]	[illegible]	[illegible]	[illegible]	[illegible]	10
	County Waterford					
[illegible]	[illegible]	[illegible]	[illegible]	[illegible]	[illegible]	[illegible]
	County Cork					
[illegible]	[illegible]	[illegible]	[illegible]	[illegible]	[illegible]	[illegible]
	County Kerry					
[illegible]	[illegible]	[illegible]	[illegible]	[illegible]	[illegible]	[illegible]
[illegible]	Do.	[illegible]	[illegible]	[illegible]	[illegible]	[illegible]
[illegible]	[illegible]	[illegible]	[illegible]	[illegible]	[illegible]	[illegible]
	County [illegible]					
[illegible]	[illegible]	[illegible]	[illegible]	[illegible]	[illegible]	[illegible]
	County [illegible]					
[illegible]	[illegible]	[illegible]	[illegible]	[illegible]	[illegible]	[illegible]
[illegible]	[illegible]	[illegible]	[illegible]	[illegible]	[illegible]	[illegible]

No. 6

1884, and substance of Reports received as to state of Rain

[illegible]	[illegible]

List of Licences to Plant Oyster Beds [illegible]

[illegible]

APPENDIX, No. 1.

No. 1—continued.

County Galway—continued.

County Mayo.

County Sligo.

County Donegal.

[illegible]	[illegible]	[illegible]	[illegible]	[illegible]	[illegible]	[illegible]
	Co. Londonderry(?)					
[illegible]	[illegible]	[illegible]	[illegible]	[illegible]	[illegible]	[illegible]
	County Down(?)					
[illegible]	[illegible]	[illegible]	[illegible]	[illegible]	[illegible]	[illegible]
[illegible]	[illegible]	[illegible]	[illegible]	[illegible]	[illegible]	[illegible]
	County Louth(?)					
[illegible]	[illegible]	[illegible]	[illegible]	[illegible]	[illegible]	[illegible]
[illegible]	[illegible]	[illegible]	[illegible]	[illegible]	[illegible]	[illegible]
[illegible]	[illegible]	[illegible]	[illegible]	[illegible]	[illegible]	[illegible]
[illegible]	[illegible]	[illegible]	[illegible]	[illegible]	[illegible]	[illegible]
[illegible]	[illegible]	[illegible]	[illegible]	[illegible]	[illegible]	[illegible]

Appendix

[illegible]

County.	[illegible]	[illegible]	[illegible]	[illegible]	[illegible]	[illegible]	[illegible]
			£ s. d.			£ s. d.	
Cork,	[illegible]	[illegible]	[illegible]	[illegible]	[illegible]	[illegible]	[illegible]
Kerry,	[illegible]	[illegible]	[illegible]	[illegible]	[illegible]	[illegible]	[illegible]
Leitrim,	[illegible]	[illegible]	[illegible]	[illegible]	[illegible]	[illegible]	[illegible]
Limerick,	[illegible]	[illegible]	[illegible]	[illegible]	[illegible]	[illegible]	[illegible]
Galway,	[illegible]	[illegible]	[illegible]	[illegible]	[illegible]	[illegible]	[illegible]
Sligo,	[illegible]	[illegible]	[illegible]	[illegible]	[illegible]	[illegible]	[illegible]
Mayo,	[illegible]	[illegible]	[illegible]	[illegible]	[illegible]	[illegible]	[illegible]
Clare,	[illegible]	[illegible]	[illegible]	[illegible]	[illegible]	[illegible]	[illegible]
Totals,	[illegible]	[illegible]	[illegible]	[illegible]	[illegible]	[illegible]	[illegible]

[illegible]

Appendix No. 6.

Table showing Loans applied for and advanced under the Sea and Coast Fisheries Fund Act during the Year ended 31st December, 18[illegible].

County.	No. of Applications.	No. of Applicants.	Amount of Loans applied for.	No. of Loans recommended.	No. of persons to whom Loans recommended.	Amount of Loans recommended.	No. of Loans actually issued.	Amount of Loans actually issued.	Loans cancelled or not proceeded(?)	
									No.	Amount(?)
			£ s. d.			£ s. d.		£ s. d.		£ s. d.
Antrim,	[illegible]	[illegible]	[illegible]	[illegible]	[illegible]	[illegible]	[illegible]	[illegible]	[illegible]	[illegible]
Cork,	[illegible]	[illegible]	[illegible]	[illegible]	[illegible]	[illegible]	[illegible]	[illegible]	[illegible]	[illegible]
Donegal,	[illegible]	[illegible]	[illegible]	[illegible]	[illegible]	[illegible]	[illegible]	[illegible]	[illegible]	[illegible]
Down,	[illegible]	[illegible]	[illegible]	[illegible]	[illegible]	[illegible]	[illegible]	[illegible]	[illegible]	[illegible]
Dublin,	[illegible]	[illegible]	[illegible]	[illegible]	[illegible]	[illegible]	[illegible]	[illegible]	[illegible]	[illegible]
Londonderry,	[illegible]	[illegible]	[illegible]	[illegible]	[illegible]	[illegible]	[illegible]	[illegible]	[illegible]	[illegible]
Louth,	[illegible]	[illegible]	[illegible]	[illegible]	[illegible]	[illegible]	[illegible]	[illegible]	[illegible]	[illegible]
Meath,	[illegible]	[illegible]	[illegible]	[illegible]	[illegible]	[illegible]	[illegible]	[illegible]	[illegible]	[illegible]
Waterford,	[illegible]	[illegible]	[illegible]	[illegible]	[illegible]	[illegible]	[illegible]	[illegible]	[illegible]	[illegible]
Wexford,	[illegible]	[illegible]	[illegible]	[illegible]	[illegible]	[illegible]	[illegible]	[illegible]	[illegible]	[illegible]
Wicklow,	[illegible]	[illegible]	[illegible]	[illegible]	[illegible]	[illegible]	[illegible]	[illegible]	[illegible]	[illegible]
Totals,	[illegible]	[illegible]	[illegible]	[illegible]	[illegible]	[illegible]	[illegible]	[illegible]	[illegible]	[illegible]

No. 4—continued.

1885, and Substance of Reports received as to state of Beds—continued.

No. of Licence	Substance of Reports received as to State of Beds
	County Londonderry.
[illegible]	No Report received.
	County Sligo(?).
[illegible]	Nothing done since last Report; beds have been abandoned as unsuccessful.
[illegible]	No Report received.
	County Louth.
[illegible]	No Report received.
[illegible]	Do.
[illegible]	Do.
[illegible]	Do.
[illegible]	Do. Licence [illegible]

No. 5.

First Act during the year 1885, and the Total Amount of Loans advanced, and Total ending 31st December, 1885.

APPENDIX No. 8.

SUMMARY of the quantity of SALMON, HERRINGS, MACKEREL, and COD, exported to undermentioned places in England, consigned from Irish Fisheries, from 1st January to 31st December, 1884.

	Salmon. No. of Boxes of 140 lbs each.	Herrings. No. of Boxes of 2 cwt. each.	Mackerel. No. of Boxes of 2 cwt. each.	Cod. No. of Boxes of 1 cwt. each.
London,	6,[illegible]	10,677	[illegible],777	7,011
Nottingham,	8,444	3,118	3,186	2,016
Bradford,	3,[illegible]	8,720	8,019	2,6[illegible]
Manchester,	7,[illegible]	11,679	3,[illegible]	7,781
Sheffield,	3,[illegible]	6,784	8,711	8,[illegible]
Wolverhampton,	8,977	5,674	4,[illegible]	2,[illegible]
Leeds,	4,[illegible]	4,[illegible]	4,310	3,1[illegible]
Liverpool,	11,311	13,810	10,[illegible]	11,1[illegible]
Birmingham,	6,070	6,[illegible]	8,974	4,[illegible]
Total, 1884,	[illegible]	79,[illegible]	[illegible]	[illegible]
" 1883,	[illegible]	76,[illegible]	[illegible],370	[illegible]
Increase,	[illegible]	2,271	[illegible]	[illegible]

			£	s.	d.
Computing Salmon at £3 [illegible] per box, the price realized in Liverpool,			1[illegible],147	15	0
" Herrings at £1	do.	do.,	79,[illegible]	0	0
" Mackerel at £1 1s.	do.	do.,	[illegible],[illegible]	16	0
" Cod at £1 [illegible]	do.	do.,	[illegible]	1[illegible]	0
Total,			£[illegible]	[illegible]	0

The quantity of Mackerel exported at the [illegible] in Ireland, mentioned at page 4, by boats belonging to the United Kingdom, so far as returns have been received, was [illegible] boxes, which realized the sum of £[illegible], at an average cost of about [illegible] per box. From many parts of the coast, however, no returns have been received.

Returns of the quantity of fish exported [illegible] have not been received.

APPENDIX No. 9.

RETURN of the Quantity of Salted and Cured Fish imported during the Year 1884.

Port.	Quantity. Tons.	Quantity. Cwts.	Quantity. Barrels.	Destination.
Baltimore,	1	—	1,437½	Ling and Herrings.
Belfast,	678	—	—	Various and Herrings.
Cork,	2,[illegible]	6	—	Do.
Drogheda,	3	7	519	Do.
Dublin,	811	—	7,[illegible]	Do.
Dundalk,	[illegible]	—	1,310	Do.
Galway,	—	—	1,277	Herrings.
Limerick,	1,[illegible]	17	—	Various and Herrings.
Londonderry,	125	—	6,[illegible]	Do.
Newry,	—	—	2,072	Herrings.
Westport,	196	16	—	Ling and Herrings.
Wexford,	—	—	[illegible]	Herrings.
Totals,	5,[illegible]	1[illegible]	21,853½	

APPENDIX, No. 10.

SCHEDULE of LICENCE DUTIES received by the BOARDS of CONSERVATORS for the Year 1885.

Districts.	[illegible]	[illegible]	[illegible]	[illegible]	[illegible]	[illegible]	[illegible]
[illegible]	[illegible]	[illegible]	[illegible]	[illegible]	[illegible]	[illegible]	[illegible]
Total,	[illegible]	[illegible]	[illegible]	[illegible]	[illegible]	[illegible]	[illegible]

APPENDIX, No. 11.

TABLE showing the Total Amount received in the various Fishery Districts from the sale of Licenses between the years 1863 and 1885, inclusive.

Year	Amount received for License Duty. £ s. d.	Year	Amount received for License Duty. £ s. d.	Year	Amount received for License Duty. £ s. d.
[illegible]	[illegible]	[illegible]	[illegible]	[illegible]	[illegible]
[illegible]	[illegible]	[illegible]	[illegible]	[illegible]	[illegible]
[illegible]	[illegible]	[illegible]	[illegible]	[illegible]	[illegible]
[illegible]	[illegible]	[illegible]	[illegible]	[illegible]	[illegible]
[illegible]	[illegible]	[illegible]	[illegible]	[illegible]	[illegible]
[illegible]	[illegible]	[illegible]	[illegible]	[illegible]	[illegible]
[illegible]	[illegible]	[illegible]	[illegible]	[illegible]	[illegible]
[illegible]	[illegible]	[illegible]	[illegible]		

Appendix, No. 13.

Schedule of License Duties payable in each District on Engines used for Fishing for Salmon, January, [illegible].

Districts.	1. [illegible]	2. [illegible]	3. [illegible]	4. [illegible]	5. [illegible]	6. [illegible]	7. [illegible]	8. [illegible]	9. [illegible]	10. [illegible]	11. [illegible]	12. [illegible]	13. [illegible]	14. [illegible]	15. [illegible]	16. [illegible]
	£ s. d.	£ s. d.	£ s. d.	£ s. d.	£ s. d.	£ s. d.	£ s. d.	£ s. d.	£ s. d.	£ s. d.	£ s. d.	£ s. d.	£ s. d.	£ s. d.	£ s. d.	£ s. d.
1. Dublin,	[illegible]	[illegible]	[illegible]	[illegible]	[illegible]	[illegible]	[illegible]						[illegible]	—	—	—
2. Wexford,	[illegible]	[illegible]	[illegible]	[illegible]	[illegible]	[illegible]	[illegible]						[illegible]	—	—	—
3. Waterford,	[illegible]	[illegible]	[illegible]	[illegible]	[illegible]	[illegible]	[illegible]						[illegible]	—	—	—
4. Lismore,	[illegible]	[illegible]	[illegible]	[illegible]	[illegible]	[illegible]	[illegible]						[illegible]	—	—	—
5. Cork,	[illegible]	[illegible]	[illegible]	[illegible]	[illegible]	[illegible]	[illegible]						[illegible]	—	—	—
[illegible] Skibbereen,	[illegible]	[illegible]	[illegible]	[illegible]	[illegible]	[illegible]	[illegible]						[illegible]	—	—	—
[illegible] Bantry,	[illegible]	[illegible]	[illegible]	[illegible]	[illegible]	[illegible]	[illegible]						[illegible]	—	—	—
[illegible] Kenmare,	[illegible]	[illegible]	[illegible]	[illegible]	[illegible]	[illegible]	[illegible]						[illegible]	[illegible]	[illegible]	—
[illegible]	[illegible]	[illegible]	[illegible]	[illegible]	[illegible]	[illegible]	[illegible]						[illegible]	—	—	—
[illegible] Limerick,	[illegible]	[illegible]	[illegible]	[illegible]	[illegible]	[illegible]	[illegible]						[illegible]	—	—	—
[illegible] Galway,	[illegible]	[illegible]	[illegible]	[illegible]	[illegible]	[illegible]	[illegible]	[illegible]	[illegible]	[illegible]	[illegible]	[illegible]	[illegible]	—	—	—
[illegible] Ballynakill,	[illegible]	[illegible]	[illegible]	[illegible]	[illegible]	[illegible]	[illegible]						[illegible]	—	—	—
[illegible] Bangor,	[illegible]	[illegible]	[illegible]	[illegible]	[illegible]	[illegible]	[illegible]						[illegible]	—	—	—
[illegible] Ballina,	[illegible]	[illegible]	[illegible]	[illegible]	[illegible]	[illegible]	[illegible]						[illegible]	—	—	—
[illegible] Sligo,	[illegible]	[illegible]	[illegible]	[illegible]	[illegible]	[illegible]	[illegible]						[illegible]	—	—	—
[illegible] Ballyshannon,	[illegible]	[illegible]	[illegible]	[illegible]	[illegible]	[illegible]	[illegible]						[illegible]	—	[illegible]	—
[illegible] Letterkenny,	[illegible]	[illegible]	[illegible]	[illegible]	[illegible]	[illegible]	[illegible]						[illegible]	—	[illegible]	[illegible]
[illegible] Londonderry,	[illegible]	[illegible]	[illegible]	[illegible]	[illegible]	[illegible]	[illegible]						[illegible]	—	—	—
[illegible] Coleraine,	[illegible]	[illegible]	[illegible]	[illegible]	[illegible]	[illegible]	[illegible]						[illegible]	—	[illegible]	—
[illegible]	[illegible]	[illegible]	[illegible]	[illegible]	[illegible]	[illegible]	[illegible]						[illegible]	—	—	—
[illegible] Drogheda,	[illegible]	[illegible]	[illegible]	[illegible]	[illegible]	[illegible]	[illegible]						[illegible]	—	[illegible]	[illegible]
[illegible] Dundalk,	[illegible]	[illegible]	[illegible]	[illegible]	[illegible]	[illegible]	[illegible]						[illegible]	—	[illegible]	—

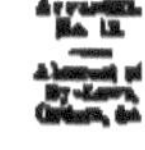

APPENDIX, No. 12.

ABSTRACT of BY-LAWS, ORDERS, &c., in force on 1st January, 1886, [illegible] the SALMON FISHERIES of IRELAND.

[illegible]	[illegible]	[illegible]	[illegible]
[illegible]	[illegible]	[illegible]	[illegible]

APPENDIX, No. 13—continued.

[illegible]

[illegible]

Appendix, No. 18—continued.

Abstract of By-Laws, Orders, &c., in force on 1st January, 1896, relating to the Salmon Fisheries of Ireland.

APPENDIX No. 13—continued.

ABSTRACT of By-Laws, Orders, &c., in force on 1st January, 1886, relating to the Salmon Fisheries of Ireland.

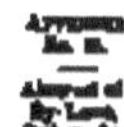

APPENDIX No. 11—continued.

ABSTRACT of BY-LAWS, ORDERS, &c., in force on 1st January, [illegible], **relating to the** SALMON FISHERIES of IRELAND.

Ballyshannon District—continued.

[illegible]

Letterkenny District.

[illegible]

Londonderry District.

[illegible]

Coleraine District.

[illegible]

Coleraine District—continued.

[illegible]

Dundalk District.

[illegible]

Drogheda District.

[illegible]

APPENDIX,

TABLE showing the Close Seasons for Salmon and Trout in [illegible]

No. and Name of District.	Limits of District.	Dates.
1. Dublin.	[illegible]	[illegible]
2. Wexford.	[illegible] Bay, East of Bannow Bay.	[illegible]
3. Waterford.	[illegible]	[illegible]
4. Lismore.	[illegible]	[illegible]
5. Cork.	[illegible]	[illegible]
6. Skibbereen.	[illegible]	[illegible]
7. Bantry.	[illegible]	[illegible]
8. Kenmare.	[illegible]	[illegible]
9. Killarney.	[illegible]	[illegible]
10. Limerick.	[illegible]	[illegible]
11. Galway.	[illegible]	[illegible]

[illegible]

No. 16

[illegible] Districts in Ireland on 31st December, 1865.

No.	[illegible]	[illegible]	[illegible]	[illegible]	[illegible]
1.	[illegible]	[illegible]	[illegible]	[illegible]	[illegible]
2.	[illegible]	[illegible]	[illegible]	[illegible]	[illegible]
3.	[illegible]	[illegible]	[illegible]	[illegible]	[illegible]
4.	[illegible]	[illegible]	[illegible]	[illegible]	[illegible]
[illegible]	[illegible]	[illegible]	[illegible]	[illegible]	[illegible]
[illegible]	[illegible]	[illegible]	Do. do.	[illegible]	[illegible]
[illegible]	[illegible]	[illegible]	[illegible]	[illegible]	[illegible]
[illegible]	[illegible]	[illegible]	[illegible]	[illegible]	[illegible]
[illegible]	[illegible]	[illegible]	[illegible]	[illegible]	[illegible]
[illegible]	[illegible]	[illegible]	[illegible]	[illegible]	[illegible]

[illegible]

APPENDIX,

TABLE showing the CLOSE SEASONS for SALMON and TROUT in

No. and Name of District	Boundary of District	Time.
[illegible]	[illegible]	[illegible] [illegible]
[illegible]	[illegible]	[illegible] [illegible]
[illegible]	[illegible]	[illegible]
[illegible] Sligo,	[illegible]	[illegible]
[illegible] Ballyshannon,	[illegible]	[illegible]
[illegible] Londonderry,	[illegible]	[illegible] [illegible] [illegible] [illegible]
[illegible]	[illegible]	[illegible]
[illegible] Coleraine,	[illegible]	[illegible] August and [illegible] February.

No. 11—continued,

the different Districts in Ireland on 31st December, 1883.

[illegible]	[illegible]	[illegible]	[illegible]	[illegible]	[illegible]
[illegible]	Same as Tidal.	Same as Netting.	[illegible]	[illegible]	[illegible]
[illegible]	Same as Tidal.	Same as Netting.	[illegible]	[illegible]	[illegible]
11	[illegible]	Same as Netting in fresh water.	[illegible]	[illegible]	[illegible]
12	Between [illegible] August and [illegible]	Same as Netting in fresh water.	[illegible]	[illegible]	[illegible]
[illegible]	Same as Tidal, [illegible]	Same as Netting.	[illegible]	[illegible]	[illegible]
[illegible]	Between [illegible]	Same as Netting.	[illegible]	[illegible]	[illegible]
[illegible]	Same as Tidal.	[illegible]	[illegible]	[illegible]	[illegible]
[illegible]	[illegible]	[illegible]	[illegible]	[illegible]	[illegible]
[illegible]	Do.	[illegible]	[illegible]	[illegible]	[illegible]
[illegible]	Same as Tidal.	Same as Netting.	[illegible]	[illegible]	[illegible]
[illegible]	Same as Tidal.	Same as Netting.	[illegible]	[illegible]	[illegible]

[illegible]

APPENDIX, No. 16.

[illegible] Tidal and Fresh Water Boundaries of which have been defined to 31st December, 1883.

River.	Boundary.	Date.	
[illegible]	[illegible] Bridge,	[illegible] June,	[illegible]
[illegible]	[illegible]	[illegible]	[illegible]
[illegible]	[illegible]	[illegible]	[illegible]
[illegible]	[illegible] Bridge	[illegible]	[illegible]
[illegible]	[illegible]	[illegible]	[illegible]
[illegible]	[illegible]	[illegible]	[illegible]
[illegible]	[illegible]	[illegible]	[illegible]
[illegible]	[illegible]	[illegible] April,	[illegible]
[illegible]	[illegible]	[illegible]	[illegible]
[illegible]	[illegible]	[illegible]	[illegible]
[illegible]	[illegible]	[illegible]	[illegible]
[illegible]	[illegible] Bridge,	[illegible]	[illegible]
[illegible]	[illegible]	[illegible] August,	[illegible]
Dee,	[illegible] Weir	[illegible] May,	[illegible]
[illegible]	[illegible]	[illegible] November,	[illegible]
[illegible]	[illegible]	[illegible] July,	[illegible]
[illegible]	[illegible]	[illegible] May,	[illegible]
[illegible]	[illegible]	[illegible] June,	[illegible]
[illegible]	[illegible]	[illegible] October,	[illegible]
[illegible]	[illegible]	[illegible] April,	[illegible]
[illegible]	[illegible]	[illegible] March,	[illegible]
[illegible]	[illegible]	[illegible] June,	[illegible]
[illegible]	[illegible]	[illegible] October,	[illegible]
[illegible]	[illegible] Bridge,	[illegible]	[illegible]
[illegible]	[illegible]	[illegible] March,	[illegible]
[illegible]	[illegible]	[illegible]	[illegible]
[illegible]	[illegible]	[illegible]	[illegible]
[illegible]	[illegible]	[illegible]	[illegible]
[illegible]	[illegible]	[illegible]	[illegible]
[illegible]	[illegible]	[illegible]	[illegible]
[illegible]	[illegible]	[illegible]	[illegible]
[illegible]	[illegible]	[illegible]	[illegible]
[illegible]	[illegible]	[illegible]	[illegible]
[illegible]	[illegible]	[illegible]	[illegible]
[illegible]	[illegible]	[illegible]	[illegible]
[illegible]	[illegible]	[illegible]	[illegible]
[illegible]	[illegible]	[illegible]	[illegible]
[illegible]	[illegible]	[illegible]	[illegible]
[illegible]	[illegible]	[illegible]	[illegible]
[illegible]	[illegible]	[illegible]	[illegible]
[illegible]	[illegible]	[illegible] April,	[illegible]
[illegible]	[illegible]	[illegible] August,	[illegible]
[illegible]	[illegible] Bridge,	1st February,	[illegible]
[illegible]	[illegible]	[illegible]	[illegible]
[illegible]	[illegible] Bridge,	[illegible] June,	[illegible]
[illegible]	[illegible]	[illegible] March,	[illegible]
[illegible]	[illegible]	[illegible] February,	[illegible]
[illegible]	[illegible] Bridge,	[illegible]	[illegible]

www.ingramcontent.com/pod-product-compliance
Lightning Source LLC
Chambersburg PA
CBHW030017030726
47499CB00008B/3030
* 9 7 8 3 7 4 2 8 1 2 3 2 2 *